Acknowledgments:

I give all thanks to God, the Author and Finisher of my faith. He gave me the gift to write. Therefore, He gets all of the credit.

I want to express my deepest appreciation to Justin K. Finch for his hard work on the illustration and the cover of this book.

I thank my children and grandsons: Keilah, Joshua, Seraya, Joy, Haliek and Ryan. I appreciate all of their encouragement and patience, while I took time away from them to complete this project. I want to thank, my very best friend and sister Cherrie Webb, for prayers and words of inspiration, as I sat hours, working on this book. I am grateful to Cassandra Allen, my media contact @ bullhorngypsy.com, who always exhibits blind faith in my abilities, which encourages me to be the best God intends. Thanks, to my Pastors: Bishop Daniel Robertson, Jr. and Elena Robertson – my mentors: Pastor Katherine Corbett, Brenda Gonzalez and Brendell Francis – my 'sisters' Patricia Ryland-Fisher, Anitrese Sadio, Kandice Corbett, Kenyatta Preston, Mary Berry, Suzanne Weathers, Kyella

Gilliam, Marilyn, Peggy Whitfield, Monique Tookes, Yvonne Pierre and Mellanese Knockett – my 'brothers' Richard "Poncho" Cabrel, Irving Brook, Jr, Carlos Brooks, Darryl Brooks, Anthony Brooks, Eddie Corbett, Jr, Frank Corbett and Kirk Knockett - the 'older women' Selma Preston and Kathleen Jones – my "other kids:" Jatajah, Shinika, and Cortnei – my nieces and nephews: Nicole, Michael, Lewis, Marianna, Marisol, Nick, Mo, Tony, David, Sylvia, Evelyn, Debra, Levone, LaToya, Nikki, Desiree, Diondre "Munch", Ashley, and Jonathan – Special recognition to those who have supported me, Tia Browne, Joanie Webb, Pamela Hancock, Helen Hinshaw and the countless others who have reassured and succored me through intercession – last, but not least, those of you who purchased this book.

LIKE A ROARING LION

BY: Inez R. Reilly

Publisher Sadie Books, 215 E Camden Ave H11, Moorestown, NJ 08057 → 856-313-0548
sadie-books.com

ISBN-10: 061-555525X
ISBN-13: 978-0615555256
Library of Congress Control No: 2011941481

Cover Art
Justin K. Finch

Book Layout / Cover Design
C Allen Design – callendesign.com

Other Published books by Inez R. Reilly

All Other Ground
How to Taste it at the End of the Day
Covenant

Media Representation
Bullhorngypsy.com

Inezreilly.com

LIKE A
ROARING LION

INEZ R. REILLY

JACQUELINE YOUNG-WELLS

The thought of walking away sent me into a tailspin. There had to be another way for this scenario to play itself out. My family and close acquaintances continued to be livid about the choices I made, however, I expect them to respect me and to be less garrulous about their discontent. It is my life; I will live or die with my decisions.

I must admit I would love a second spin at the wheel of life. Perhaps I would have recognized the signs and sought counsel earlier. I would have had discussions when loved ones and friends attempted to raise the subject of my relationship. Instead, I closeted myself within my fairytale walls and kept silent. Sure, there were times I toyed with the idea that someone would understand. Yet, I was more convinced I would be judged and ridiculed.

I accused my family of bigotry, when they first approached me about my marriage. I could not hear their words for the racial slurs I heard in their voices. My father wanted me to marry one of the deacons in church, one who could understand my background; someone who could assist in raising children and who could respect the boundaries that exist in the populace. He thought he had instilled those values in me and I am haunted by the repugnance in his eyes. I chose my husband, a tall, beautiful and intelligent African American.

I wanted to believe that racism was dead, in the Commonwealth. I was taken aback as I listened to my father beg me to not degrade myself; not to lower the standards that he and my mother had established for my sister, brother and I; not to marry black trash. He told me my children would never be accepted in the world and they would struggle, unnecessarily, and it would be my fault. When I asked if *he* would feel that way about *my* children, he huffed and stormed out of the room, insisting that my mother try to talk some sense into me.

I pleaded with my father, just before my wedding day, to walk me down the aisle. But, my pleas fell on deaf ears. He refused to be a part of me 'destroying my life' as he liked to put it. So, I marched toward the altar on my own. Tears on my cheeks, I glanced at the bride's side of the church that was eerily vacant. At the rehearsal, I informed the minister that there would be no need to ask, 'Who gives this bride, in marriage?' as there would be no one there to respond. He stared blankly, at first, and then nodded his head in assent. I breathed a sigh of relief, the moment we got past that portion of the ceremony.

I was strengthened by love and adoration I saw in my husband's eyes, as he recited his vows. He was blessed to have me to choose him; he is, and will continue to be, a better man because he has me to stand by his side; he loved me with adoration beyond understanding; he would be able to face anything because he and I would face it, together.

He lied.

I stood looking out of the window of our condominium, absentmindedly. All of my thoughts were scattered, refusing to form a cohesive picture. I could see the trees billowing as the never-ending winds raced through their branches. I noticed a wintry mix falling from the sky and laughed as I realized it resembled the feeling within my heart. There was no humor in the simile; amusement was more evil than anything. I glanced at the deadbolt lock on the door and the missing key crossed my mind.

Returning my gaze to the naked limbs on the trees, tears began to make a path down my face. With each passing day, I experienced more despondency than joy. I could feel my spirit looking for a deeper place to fall. The ideation of digging a pit that has no end moved stealthily into my subconscious. Images of me shoveling aside the earth of my essence created inexpressible pain, as I lie in an indention of myself.

When I was younger I was mindful of my potential. I set goals, for myself, and there was nothing that kept me from racing to my dreams. I excelled in my academic career. After obtaining a Bachelor Degree in Life Science, I volleyed for the perfect internships and furthered my education to achieve my Masters Degree, all of which paid off with a job, as a Microbiologist for the Virginia Department of Health, in Chesapeake. I was in charge of controlling and testing mosquito pools for Eastern

Equine Encephalitis, sleeping sickness to the layperson. I inoculated samples into tissue cultures for virus screening and developed lab protocols, and I reported specimen-testing results to local mosquito control boards. To most, my profession resonates mind numbingly tiresomeness. However, it was my life's joy.

A painful childhood experience fueled my passion for my profession. Back then; my family owned a few horses and we secured them at one of the local stables. I loved riding my chocolate-speckled mare, Misty, every opportunity I could get. After an unusually rainy season, there was a rise in mosquito population, in the Chesapeake Bay area. My parents took my siblings and me to the stable to check on the horses. I noticed Misty seemed drowsy, her ears drooped and she circled aimlessly. I ran to the stable master and he quickly dismissed me. I hurried to my father and we rushed to the yard where Misty wandered about, unsteadily and seemingly unaware.

My father immediately called a veterinarian to ask for an emergency visit. We waited, anxiously, for the hour and a half it took him to arrive, and then we escorted him to Misty's stable. After his examination, we were told Misty was suffering from Eastern Equine Encephalitis. She was at advanced stage of disease, which was caused by the bite of an infected mosquito. Misty also had lesions, covering her brain, causing symptoms. He advised they would worsen until she was completely paralyzed, and then death would follow.

I remember crying and crying as it was becoming clear the best option was to have Misty euthanized. My father, mother, sister, brother and I held each other's hands, while Dr. Matthews administered the lethal dose of barbiturates. Misty lost consciousness, and then later died from the overdose. I recall how still we stood watching her draw her last breath. It was then I vowed to do my best to never have another person endure that heartache.

Thinking of Misty gave my tears purpose, as I watched the rain and sleet mix to sheet the ground, I allowed my liquid pain to fall unchecked until it soaked the front of my shirt. My mother talked about our tears being collected, in a bottle, by God. I imagined God being overloaded with my honeyed prayers; then wondered why they went unanswered. My father preached God acknowledged every petition. What made my pleas less significant? I mused, what could be more pressing than my aching soul? Whose beseeching had topped mine, requiring His immediate attention, leaving my pleas to fall to the ground?

I was roused from my reverie, as I realized I needed to call my job to advise that I would not make it in, today. I walked into the bedroom, retrieved my cell phone, and I dialed the numbers, slowly. I waited, as the call connected.

"Hello, the Virginia Department of Health, Danielle speaking."

"Hello, Danielle, it's Jacqueline Wells." I know my voice sounded drab and tired.

"Jacqueline, you sound awful and sick?"

"Yeah, I am not feeling well, at all. I must be coming down with the flu bug that is going around the office." I lied.

"I am sorry to hear that. Are you crying? Do you feel that badly?" I could hear the concern in Danielle's voice.

"I have been crying, but I will be okay. I am not sure if I will make it, at all, this week." Unfortunately, that was the truth.

"Well, it is best for you to take care of yourself, before the bug is spread further. I will tell everyone. Feel better soon, Jacqueline. And, let us know if you need anything." Danielle disconnected the line.

I sat down on the bed, after placing my phone on the nightstand. I exhaled. I was grateful I was not questioned further. I could not elaborate on the situation. I was not physically sick, as I had stated. I was positive distress and depression did not qualify as a legitimate ailment for calling out of work. I hope I will never have to "stretch the truth" anymore, at work.

Since I do not watch television, as a rule, I decided to search the CD case for some music. I did not want to cry, anymore. I had no one to blame, but myself. I allowed myself to get and remain in this situation. It seems God thought it best that I simmer in my stew. If that is not the case, the alternative is much worse; I had become spiritually deaf to the voice of God and there was no way I was going to be able to heed His direction.

I found what I had been searching for, in my CD collection, placed the disc in the player and stretched on the bed. My hair fell over the pillow, onto the comforter. The tunes filled the air, as I inhaled. I wanted to breathe in the peace I heard coming from the chords and the voice. My soul ached to have the experience that the singer was describing in the lyrics.

"...As the waters overflow my soul, my God will protect me. When life's circumstances seek to pull me under, the Shepherd leads me to safety..."

I searched my heart for a sign of kindred association with the song, only to find it estranged. I wanted faith to uphold me, yet it failed. I did not feel the Shepherd's leading; I felt abandoned, and alone. In that moment, I heard this audible voice, from an unknown place.

"Give all your worries and cares to God, because He cares for you."

"What?"

"Give all your worries and cares to God, because He cares for you."

Without care as to how insane I sounded, I replied, "What does that mean? I have been praying and asking God to help me, without answer."

"Indeed the words left your lips, yet they did not originate from your heart. Yes, I know you believe your heartache should have been enough to compel God to move. Yet, you never believed He cared about you." I could not decipher if the voice was male or female. It just was a voice.

A great sense of condemnation took me.

"That is not from God." The enigma stated, matter-of-factly.

"What is not from God? I asked.

"Self-effacing guilt and shame is not from God and should not be entertained."

"Are we really given enough information to discern what is God and what is not, when it comes to our feelings?"

"Feelings that satisfy your flesh's desire to feel good or bad are not spiritually useful. God's intent is to draw you closer to Him, for you to be healed from the result of the decisions you make, outside of His will; and for you to enhance upon the faith that is fostered when you choose His way over your own."

"So, in my case, you are saying that I do not believe God wants to give me answers I seek?" I heard the incredulousness in my own voice.

"You are asking the questions, and instead of expecting God to instruct you, you are relying on the past experiences to come up with a solution."

First, I did not consider what I was hearing could be the truth. I did not want to think that my lack of response was my onus. It is much easier to blame the unknown, than to accept responsibility for the length of my melancholy. However, I was not able to deny it.

"But as many as received Him, to them He gave the right to become children of God, to those who believe in His name."

"Yeah, yeah, yeah." I stated. "I get what you are saying. I have to make my calling an election sure, as my father used to say. I have to come to God, believe that He is and that He rewards those who diligently seek Him." I closed my eyes, as realization came upon like a flood.

"Now, there is no condemnation to those who are in Christ." The voice comforted.

"I hear you."

"For God so loved the world that He gave His only begotten Son, that whosoever believes in Him will not perish, but have everlasting life. He did that for everyone, including you, Jacqueline."

"I know that."

"He did that for you, Jacqueline. He so loved Jacqueline that He gave His only begotten Son. Believe it, Jacqueline, and you will not perish. The essence of who you are will not perish, but live forever."

I felt something in the pit of my stomach. A chill, without the cold, permeated me and I knew. I sighed, as tears fell down my face, afresh. "Why couldn't you have come to me, before I married him?" My tears were now sobs. "Why now?"

"But there is far more to life for us. We're citizens of high heaven! We're waiting the arrival of the Savior and Master, Who will transform our earthly bodies into glorious bodies like His own. He'll make us beautiful and whole with the same powerful skill by which He is putting everything as it should be, under and around Him." There was a sense of urgency in the voice. "Let's not linger on the 'whys' of the matter."

"Ok, no time for questions. I get that, right now." I trembled. My heart was troubled. There was so much I wanted; so many words left unspoken; so many tasks that will remain undone; so many dreams that will not be realized.

The voice was speaking; but, I missed the first part. "I go to prepare a place for you. And if I go and prepare a place for you, I will come again and receive you to myself; that where I am, there you may be also."

"Yeah." I could not muster up the strength to say anything. Fear assailed me.

"Do not be afraid, Jacqueline. For the Lord will not cast you off, neither forsake you."

A laugh of derision escaped. I laughed, like a madwoman. My father had forsaken me and left me to myself. How could I believe that God would want me?

"God is not man that He would lie. If He said it, He will do it. He promises to never leave you to yourself or devises. He loves you, unconditionally. His love never fails. He wants you and He always has. You can believe that; trust it."

Oddly enough, fear was being quelled by calming effect of the voice. I felt serene, deep within my spirit, a quiet I had not experienced, in my life. I trusted the voice and I believed what was being said to me.

I was so engrossed; I had not realized that someone had come into the house. I heard footsteps rush down the hall, as if to catch someone. Suddenly, he burst into the room, barreling at me, with fists balled up.

Before I could speak, my voice was cut off, violently, as my attacker's clenched hand connected with my mouth. My body shook from terror. My mind reeled, confused; dumfounded. I had questions, but there was no way to verbalize them, as the assault grew more vicious.

My assailant grabbed the collar of my shirt, snatching me up from the bed and onto my feet. He slapped me, open-handed, this time. I could feel blood stream from my lip and a cut under my eye. He pushed me against the wall. His eyes were crazed.

He screamed unintelligible words into the air and his spittle sprayed on my face. He slammed me against the wall, once more.

"What are you doing here?" My voice was barely a whisper. I could feel my lips, as they were swelling, making it difficult to formulate words. I felt my ribs crack, after an added punch to my midsection. The pain was searing and causing my breaths to be labored. Another thesis came to mind; a broken rib could puncture my lung. I tried to scramble, to get out of harm's way, only to feel the heel of his boot as it came down on my back. The force of the kick was crushing. I felt my muscles begin to spasm, in an attempt to protect my spine from the onslaught.

I could not imagine why I was attacked. I was petrified, with fear. I could not move. He pulled me up by my hair, from the floor. He spit in my face. His knee met my pelvic area, and then my stomach, which caused me to vomit. As I retched, I could sense his tension rising, as he grabbed hold of my collar, once more. His grip grew tighter. My breaths became shallow. I felt myself become lightheaded. The thought of rape crossed my mind. Oddly enough, it did not concern me. I had been raped, before. I felt deadened to the idea. The beating was worse than any I endured, worse than a sexual assault.

I knew I was drawing my last breaths. As I looked, intently, into my murderer's eyes, I mouthed just one word, "Why?"

Just before darkness overcame, I heard the soothing comfort of the unisex voice and then I was infused with peace. "In My Father's house there are many mansions. If it were not so, I would have told you. Do not be afraid."

And I wasn't.

KENNETH YOUNG

Sitting in the office, located on the second floor of our home, I watched the weather whip on the other side of the window. The wind and sleet battled for control, and the wind seemed to be triumphant. The wind's force drove bitter ice crystals wherever it decided. The scene played out like the war taking place within my soul and spirit. One wanted its way, while the other fought heatedly against it. In my profession, there should be an obvious winner, however the strength of resolve rested on one side.

My will refused to give any ground to my spirit. I recalled an old saying, 'the spirit is willing, but the flesh is weak.' In my case, the flesh rose up with a might of Samson, seeking to dominate my spirit; crush it into submission. Thus, what should have been a short-lived meeting, at best, raged on.

I heard the telephone ring, in the distance. I knew my wife would pick up the line, leaving me to my quiet sulking, unless it was important. I sighed, as I sat back in my burgundy leather chair. Its high back and cushioned arms were great support.

My wife, frequently, found me asleep while reclining in this very seat. I imagined the call would be from my daughter, begging for forgiveness and seeking to come home. In truth, I replayed the hopeful thought like a flashcard, every time the phone rang the past year or so.

My mind pushed rewind, more often than I gave it license. I did not want to relive the moments prior to my daughter throwing her life away with *that* man. I wanted a ceasefire, but my pride would not allow me to be the first to bend. She should have obeyed my command and cut the unholy relationship before things went too far. Instead, she rebelled. She snubbed her nose at this family, to take up with trash. I wanted more for her, for all of my children. I instilled godly character and qualities into them and expected them to respect me enough to follow my rules and govern their lives accordingly.

I remember the first time my children were subject to the blacks and their influence. There was a family, which found it their mission in life to distract me from my work, every Sunday. They walked into the sanctuary, as if they were welcomed. I do not understand how they did not feel scorn from the congregation when they stepped into the church. The spirit was sucked right out of the atmosphere, as they appeared.

Many fellow pastorate buds came around to a more liberal approach to allowing the blacks into their flock. They spouted about God not being a respecter of persons. I did not want to hear them defame the word of God. It was easy for them to misread the bible as it suited them and their weekly offering. I would not degrade myself, as they had done. I believe in separatism. I did not want the seed to take root, before my eyes. I did everything in my power to dissuade blacks from returning to church, yet they remained like the thorn in Paul's flesh. I could feel the bile of disgust rising in my belly, as it did every week since they insisted on taking up space that could have been used by a more suitable parishioner.

I took a deep breath, to quell unrest within my soul. I needed to concentrate on the task, completing a sermon for this week's lesson. It is imperative the 'unwanted' get the picture and never return. So, my topic, this week, would be about servants who obey masters who rule over them. I want them to walk away with the full gist of the word; they will be able to serve the Lord better, being complacent, and compliant with those who outrank them and who are in higher authority; like the members of my church.

As it was, I could not really concentrate. A memory was vying for my attention. It had been whittling away at the wall that I built around it. A nightmare came here, a vague recollection there; small chips were falling to the floor of my mind. My wife would shake me, to awaken me, as I thrashed about in bed. I did not want to remember. I would, forcibly, close my eyes and will them to remain in the dark. However, a piercing light shined on the wall, never allowing me the peace of not knowing.

My mind went back to my formative years. I could not have been more than fifteen or sixteen years old. I would hear a soft voice speaking to me through the meadow, just behind our home. A slight southern drawl made the words dance in the air. I felt a deep longing, within my soul, whenever I would hear the distinctly feminine lilt. I wanted to reach through manicured shrubs and touch the owner of the voice. I wanted to feel her skin, smell her hair, and look into her eyes. I could hardly breathe. Then, I would feel I was being suffocated. The hand clasped my throat, tighter and tighter. My eyes bulged, at the pressure. Panic surged through my entire body, as I entertained the thought that I was being strangled to death.

I wrestled my assailant. I heard footsteps hurrying away, on the other side of the foliage, as my eyes rested on my attacker. Fear and confusion gripped my mind, as I realized who it is. It is at this moment, in the dream, I feel my wife's hands gently coax me out of the vision. There would be sweat on my brow and pillow. My pajamas would be moist with perspiration. I could feel my eyes still straining from the force of strangulation. My wife would speak to me, softly. She rubbed my forehead and wiped sweat beads from my temple.

As I sat here, I felt blood coursing through my veins at an accelerated rate; my heart pounded. I could not fathom what caused disturbance, in my body. I did not know who the female presence is, in my dreams, nor do I know the antagonist. There were days that I wanted to summon up mental pictures that invaded my slumber, yet they remained elusive and vague.

I readjusted myself to refocus, in my cozy office chair. But, I could senses the chisel at work in my soul. There was no phrase I could use to assist me, as I had no idea what was trying to break forth. I pondered giving in to memory. 'How bad could it be,' I thought. There was nothing from my past that could hurt me or cause me shame; at least, not that I could call to mind.

I did not feel comfortable haggling with my subconscious. The musings of a tired man were not to be considered. My dreams and aspirations were at a brink of realization and I did not want anything to dampen the moment. Sure, I would love for my entire family to be there as the clergy recognized me, in a couple of months. Yet, we cannot always have things the way we want them. There are things and people that must be sacrificed, on our way to obtain goals. In my case, the person is my daughter. I was not going to let rebellious tirades distract me from my mission. Her argumentative behavior was not going to be given room to breed further disturbance in this home. Her insurrection would be nipped in the bud. If her dishonor and disrespect were not addressed in an infancy stage, it would blossom into full-blown anarchy.

I thought back to when my daughter was born. We had so many hopes and plans for her. As she was still in her mother's womb, we studied the best schools and nannies. We were not holding back; cost did not concern us. We wanted the best for her.

When Jacqueline was born, I cried. Purity, in her eyes, placed a resolve in my soul; I was going to do everything to give her what she deserved. There was much we had to instill in her. We would nurture and raise her with great values and self-worth. She would be proud to be whom God had created her to be, an elitist. She would hold her head high, with dignity, because she could. She was graced with birth in the favored race; she would never have to be ashamed of who she was or what she was to become.

I would speak to her, night and day, of her beauty. Jacqueline's porcelain skin likened freshly squeezed milk. She was flawless. I constantly told her how blessed she was to be born and how much we adored her. I created songs about her and how much better she was than colored counterparts. She would never endure the hardships accompanying blacks, because she was not like them. Her mind was superior to theirs and she would someday understand they were not good enough to speak to her.

When our child suckled my wife's breast, I marveled; their skin seemed like mirrored images, of each other. My daughter's pink lips met her mother's alabaster bosom, causing a stir within me. Friends would say they felt jealousy twinges when catching glimpses of wives feeding their children. I did not feel that way. I savored moments, like secret fantasies. I felt erections, more than once, while enjoying the sweet vision. There were times when I sat at my wife's feet and touched her, during the feedings. I would close my eyes and imagine things; things I would never tell a soul. I would breathe in her sweet scent. She smelled of jasmine blossoms; my daughter smelled like rose petals after rain, intoxicating.

The pain coursed through my body, when Jacqueline came to me with her decision to marry someone beneath her. It was as if she had taken a soldering iron to my eyes. I was blinded with fury, disgust and a host of emotions. I wanted to strike and kill her for destroying our dreams. The rage and torment seared an ineffaceable path in my heart. The idea of a black sickened me. Her flawless skin touched by the hands of a nigger seemed like bestiality. I could not reconcile her choice with the way she had been raised. It didn't make sense. I could not rationalize it or come to terms with it. In fact, I refused to give it a thought. I sent her from sight and told her not to return until she repented. She ran, crying, out of my office and she did not return until the next day.

I recalled positioning myself for pleas of absolution. I expected her to see the error of her ways and say she regained control of her senses. Instead, she stood resolute and more determined. She reasoned with and begged me to understand and give her my blessing. I refused. She held ground. I could not believe I was in standoff with my child, flesh and blood. How dare she face me on behalf of a low-life miscreant! I was appalled. She was in love. I could find no leverage or niche for my assault, because she refused to give in. I stormed out of the room, bellowing for her mother, insisting she go to the room and bring her to sense.

I heard her mother cry and plead with her. She did all she could to compel Jacqueline to recall all she was taught. There was no reason to search amongst the dregs of the earth to find a companion; there were men within our flock from good and upstanding families, within the community. If she did not find a mate, in church, there were other churches where she could choose a mate. Our daughter would not give ear to us. She cried and remained defiant.

Her sister and brother listened from a hall, across the breezeway. I could hear Rachel and Pernell whispering, to one another. Rachel argued they should have a right to choose whomever they felt the right one; while Pernell agreed with the consensus of his parents. At least one of them got the message and was stalwart in the paradigm that ruled the household. I made a mental note to speak with my youngest daughter about the hellish notion breeding within. I would not allow contempt of everything we held dear. We needed to be a cohesive unit, if we were to stand against the wiles of the enemy. I knew this hell-raiser had infiltrated my daughter's mind and I would be damned, if I would allow him to hold her hostage with his lies.

My wife, Sarah emerged from the study, shaken from the experience. She looked at me, and shook her head, as her body shook with her sobs. I slammed my hand down on the table in the foyer, causing the flower-filled vase to fall and shatter on the granite floor. My wife screamed, and then hurried up the stairs to the bedroom. I heard my children rush to their rooms and close their doors, at the same moment Jacqueline stepped out of the room. There were no tears, just abject sadness in her eyes. I didn't want to look at her, but I could not turn away. Her back was erect and her gorgeous hair, the color of raven feathers, fell delicately on her shoulders.

She looked imperial. I was taken aback at her beauty. It was in that moment rage consumed me, and I did not realize I was moving until I was standing, directly, in front of her. Before I could stop myself (perhaps I did not want to), I raised my hand to slap her.

I felt exhilarated. I wanted to beat sense back into her. She screamed and cowered down, to stave off blows. I could not stop. I did not want her beauty to be marred by another. In my crazed state, I preferred to do the marring. I did not want her to be appealing to this black man. I wanted him to detest her, like I detested him.

Pernell grabbed my hand. I heard him beg me to stop. He implored me to remember that Young men do not hit their women. It was beneath us to demean or cause them harm. I wrestled with him, yet he would not let me go until my hands rested at my side. I was exhausted. I was hurt. I could not stand the sight of Jacqueline, as long as she spent her life with someone akin to a primate. I ordered her to leave and then turned my back. I walked to my office and closed the door, just as Jacqueline closed the front door of our home.

The doorbell stirred me from memories. I rose from my chair to look out the window. I noticed two police cars in the driveway. I headed toward the door, when I heard my wife cry out. I hurried to make my way down the stairs to see what was causing the commotion. I noticed three officers, two male and one female, standing in the foyer. The woman was holding my wife, trying to keep her upright.

One of the male officers noticed me, and asked if I was Kenneth Young. I nodded my head. His partner approached me and gave me the news. Jacqueline Wells was brutally murdered. They found her, on the floor in one of the bedrooms of her home. I felt the room spin and sat on the bottom step, so I would not fall to the floor. I could not believe my ears. An animal had murdered my beloved angel. The untamed hands of an assailant shattered a precious porcelain doll. Fury filled my stomach and a dark rage saturated my spirit. I heard a blood-curdling scream, in the distance. It sounded like my youngest, Rachel. She must have been near when the officer told us that my Jacqueline was dead.

I raised myself from a step and I walked to my wife. I took her in my arms and held her close. The devastating news was more than she could grasp. I felt her equilibrium collapse as she gave way to the darkness. She fell limp and I lifted her body, pulling her to me. Pernell raced to his sister's side, just before she fainted. Hysteria set in and there was nothing I could do.

The officers stood, aloof. I understood they delivered news like this often. I imagined the scene unfolding, in front of them was not uncommon. Yet, it wasn't supposed to be playing out in my house. They should not be here, with unemotional stances. I wanted them to leave. We wanted to be alone. We did not want gory details of my daughter's murder. All I wanted to hear was the beast had been put down. *I* know that black, she married, had something to do with it. I could feel it in my gut.

The female officer told me they had taken my son-in-law down to the precinct. Morris was in custody and being questioned, as a person of interest. I shook my head. I wanted to hear them tell me this man was dead, too. I did not want to hear he was breathing air that I was breathing. One of the male officers said he understood where I came from. I was not sure he did. I could not comprehend why he had breath when my daughter was lying dead on a slab. My mind refused to wrap around the concept that Morris Wells was alive and well, after succinctly accomplishing the destruction of my daughter.

MORRIS WELLS, JR.

I sat at the police station, with hustle and bustle about me, yet it seemed ethereal. I had no recollection of what transpired that had me sitting here, in handcuffs. I was left to brew, I imagine, by officers. They asked me questions about my wife and our relationship. *What business is it of theirs,* I asked? The officers glared, in my direction, and continued with a barrage of questions. I called my brother, Keyvaughn. He had lawyers on his payroll. He assured me this matter would be taken care of, before nightfall. I trusted him. I had no choice.

There was something I should be recalling; yet it eluded me, like an eel. Each time it came within reach, it writhed beyond my grasp. One of the officers repeatedly asked me about the bruises on my hands. I attempted to look at them, forgetting my hands were locked behind me. I wished someone would tell me what was going on. The officers returned to the room and sat at the table, across from me.

"Mr. Wells, tell us what happened before you killed your wife." The taller of the two police officers spoke.

"What?" I answered. It was difficult for me to formulate thoughts and process what was being asked of me.

"Mr. Wells, your wife is dead and you were the only other person in the house." This time, the short cop addressed me.

"What happened to innocent until proven guilty? Besides, I left my wife home, while I went to work, this morning."

"Mr. Wells, we are going to need for you to concentrate."

"I want to concentrate and assist you. My mind is foggy." I shook my head.

I wriggled my fingers; they were sore and swollen. I remembered that Jacqueline and I had an altercation the night before. I hit her. She cried. I remember the absence of sadness, on my part, at my wife's tears. I hadn't realized I had hit her so hard.

"Is this about the tiff my wife and I had, last night?"

"Tell us about it." There was something in his voice I could not put my finger on. He was making me angry.

"I welcome you taking the accusatory tone out of your voice, Mr. Officer." This cop would not speak to me, condescendingly.

"The change of tone will come from you, Mr. Wells." The officer stood up and placed his hand on a revolver. "Now, start talking about the tiff."

I could feel indignation rise in me. It was happening more, lately. I had much on my plate. My job was increasingly demanding and so was Jacqueline. I did not feel supported and she was becoming more independent. She didn't need me, like she did when she wanted to escape from her father's house. Her job was her passion, instead of me. She was more concerned about those damned mosquitoes, and her research, than she was about how stressful my line of work could be.

I have a degree in Chemical Engineering and a high-paying career. I work with chemicals and the way they interact within the environment. I create guidelines for buildings capable of housing chemicals, without polluting environment. I deal with chemists and assistants, along with over-inflated egos, while helping them package and house their prized possessions. Each one hopes and wishes to discover a new chemical compound that may save the world; or at least. They are narcissistic and hard to deal with. Now, this cop is talking to me like I am a sniveling little kid.

"I will await my attorney, and I am done talking to the both of you." I did not have to contend with a false sense of bravado. I am not easily frightened or intimidated. I sat back, trying to look more comfortable than I was feeling, and stared past them.

The officers left the room. I was relieved to be alone. My frustration levels were at the boiling point. I did not have the patience to deal with people who were puffed up with self-importance. I was sure I made more money than their salaries, combined. How dare they take a tone of elitism? I am an accomplished, intelligent man of color. I am beneath no one.

I no longer cared what circumstances had me in this situation. Whatever happened to Jacqueline, I was sure she earned it. Over time, I began to notice her conversations become tinged with the bigotry she was raised to display. I could see it in her eyes. She didn't respect me, as the head of our household. There were days I came home and she did not have dinner on the table and my beer in hand, waiting at the door. When I addressed her insubordination, she told me she had been working late. This excuse was used, too often. I didn't hear apology in her voice; instead, she looked justified in the notion her job was more important than what I wanted.

I hated it when Jacqueline approached me after we had a disagreement trying to get me to talk about what transpired. I would get furious, all over again. I told her to find it within herself to live in the moment. Once time has passed, it is gone, forever, never to be recaptured. We are to accept the present, fully. I remembered hearing an old person say God wants us to forget things behind and reach out to the future. Although, I am not into spiritual mumbo jumbo, I took that creed and applied it to my life. It's a good mantra.

I tried to see out of the small window at the police station. I couldn't see anything. They had my feet shackled to the legs of a chair, so I could not stand up. I felt like a leashed animal. I was tired of sitting in here. I wanted those bastards to come and loosen me, so I could go home. I knew Jacqueline had to be concerned about me. At least, she better be concerned. I locked her in the house, this morning, so she could think about her actions; she could mull it over, since she liked to relive things, so much. I did not appreciate being disrespected, under my own roof. I had enough to deal with, at work and with Keyvaughn. I should not have to come home to questions and menial chitchat, while I wait for dinner to be placed on the table. I bet she will do what is right, from now on, after I handled her.

Again, broken memories worked to the forefront of my mind. The cops pulled me from my house, dragging me in handcuffs. Flashes of light and color zipped across my psyche. Adrenaline pumped my veins. I felt a sense of foreboding, deep within me. Perspiration beaded across my brow. What the hell was going on? Had police officers drugged me? I wanted answers, yet I could not devise the questions. Something was going on and I was feeling desperate to know what it was.

"Get yourself together!" I could hear a voice, in my head. "You are a Wells! Man up and stop panicking!" The bête noire rebuked me, as it had done times before.

I needed to reclaim composure, to stave off mental attack. I inhaled through my nose. I exhaled from my mouth. I refused to give in and allow myself to lose control. Chinese holistic health exercises and deep breathing techniques taught me emotions and breathing have reciprocal relationship. The instructor had me to pay attention to when I panicked or felt anxious. I realized my breathing sped up and became erratic. When relaxed and composed, breathing is slow, calm and rhythmical. Through the reading and practical aspects of training, I mastered control of breathing, therefore bringing my mind and emotions into a state of stillness.

I sat still as I could. This exercise worked best, with my hands on my lap. That was not an option, so I made due. I continued to inhale for 4 seconds, hold for 7 seconds, and then exhale for 8 seconds. I paused, briefly, and then repeated. I willed myself to experience the quietude of tranquility. I could feel my mind become calmer and my emotions regain balance. I did not know what was going on, but I would not allow my emotions to run amuck. I would feel, on purpose, and respond, in a controlled manner, not react to the taunting jibes of police officers. Reacting to situations can prove to be a man's downfall. My father and Keyvaughn were sure to instill that in me. I was never to get myself drawn into another person's web, thus causing me to lash out in order to keep myself from being harmed. My mother would chime in, with her soft southern drawl.

"When you respond, you control exchange. You can choose to concede or capture. Responding keeps the balance tipped, ever so slightly, in your favor." She smiled. "Never forget this, Morris. A Wells will never be caught reacting to a situation; we play both sides of the ball. As the situation unfolds itself, we take the side that best suits our purpose. When we must, we will be on offense, capture the ball and score, in a manner that will benefit this family. When we are on defensive, we take a very unforgiving stance."

"We look to take the quarterback out, at all times." Keyvaughn took up the football analogy. "We always think blitz."

"The ball is in the wrong hands, if it isn't in our hands. Our mission is to crush the will and confidence of opponents." My father enjoyed the group lesson. "We cannot do that, if we fall prey to demands of others, or be suckered into believing the opposing team has the upper hand."

"We work best, within the two-minute drill and the red zone." My mom was excited.

"This is when our opponent believes they have us where they want." I added. "They get cocky and overzealous. They are prone to mistakes, when they can see their goal within reach."

"That is right, Morris. It is in this moment, that our response will outweigh a reaction to the obvious." My father leaned in close. "We know there is a weak link, in every chain, no matter how strong it appears. We are calm, as we look our opponent in the eye. Our training is to see the one who is skittish or who appears overbearing. We hone in and respond to their trigger." His voice is barely above a whisper. We are all locked, as he compels us with his posture. "Without knowledge or comprehension, we have thwarted their plans, rendered them ineffective. We leave them bewildered and beaten, every time."

"People who react are defeated. Reactions form once something has been done. We get reactions when we put water on fire. Each element remains its own, until one is put upon by the other." Keyvaughn stated.

I was grateful for the recollection. It aided in my quest to regain composure and quiet the demon within. I would not submit. I would rule this day, as I have others. It is my lot in life, as a Wells man, to always come out on top. We never assume a defeatist stance or take on its tone.

So, as I sat in the police station being held for questioning, I gained resolve. The cops thought they were breaking me down. In reality, I was being built up, strengthened, if you will. No matter what the outcome, there will come a time when the cards will be put on the table. And once that had been done, I would rake in the full pot. I was born into a family with a 'winner takes all' mentality. We caused reactions; simply occupying space puts others off balance.

When the cops returned, I was calm and in charge. I smiled, as they took their seats.

"What can I do for you, officers? Has my counsel arrived?"

"No, your *counsel* hasn't arrived."

"We have nothing to say to one another. Why have you returned?" I was curious to what went through their minds.

"We want to give you another opportunity to come clean." The officer dropped the formality, assuming a more personal tone.

Briefly, I wrestled unknowns; thinking they knew something I didn't. Just as quickly, the idea passed. It didn't matter what they think. It didn't even matter I had no clue what was going on. What did matter was I would never yield to attempts to throw me off course.

"Officers, I have nothing to say to you. I have no desire to come clean, as there is no dirt on my hands. I have nothing to hide or fear from you. So, unless you have something you want to say to me, there is nothing more to discuss." My eyes moved from one to the other.

"There may be no dirt, as you put it. But, there is a matter of bruises. The victim, was found bludgeoned and strangled, in your home. I know you know something about that, now don't you, Morris?" The officer taunted.

"We are prepared to hold you, for as long as we can, until you give us answers we want." The smaller cop added.

"I am prepared to speak with my attorney, once he passes through those doors. Until then, you can talk, accuse and try to cajole me into impeaching myself, all to no avail. I am not a frightened kid you picked up off the street. I am an upstanding citizen of the community. You will get a lawsuit, not the trial you seek." I loved the looks on their faces.

"Mr. Wells, I assure you we will get what we want, one way or another." The taller cop stood, while the smaller one walked to the door and stood with his arms folded.

"We know what you did, Morris." The one by the door stated, while looking out of the small opening.

The officer walked to the side of the table, where I sat. I knew what was going to happen, before he raised his fist. I braced myself for the punch and the subsequent falling off the chair. My head hit the floor, with a thud. I was unwavering, and I was conditioned to endure more. The officer knelt down, beside me, with his face close to mine.

"Did she beg you to stop?" He punched me in the abdomen.

I was brawny in my steadfastness. I was not going to crumble. "Mr. Officer, my wife begs me to do many things, but to stop is never one of them." I smiled.

"You, filthy piece of trash." He spat out, as he raised his hand for another blow.

The short cop cleared his throat and I was promptly pulled upright, again. My invader wrestled a handkerchief from his pocket, to wipe the trickle of blood that sat on my lip. He returned it to his pocket, before my lawyer walked into the room. Keyvaughn, my brother, was close on his heels.

KEYVAUGHN WELLS

As the oldest son and child of Patricia and Morris Wells, I take great pride in taking care of and managing the familial unit. My father is mentor and hero. He is supreme head of family. He taught me everything about moral code of ethics and conduct governing our family. My training started when my feet hit the floor, every morning, since I can remember. It was special time, together. He taught me rudiments of the paradigm ruling our family. When Mo was born, Dad drilled into me the importance of protecting younger siblings; I became responsible for teaching him what I had been taught. I loved the honor of being in charge and I still do.

My brother and sisters depend on me, all the while standing in their own strength. I know that is as an oxymoron, however it is how our family functions. Our first line of defense is our power. When assistance is needed, we rely on each other to structure an impenetrable powerhouse. The Wells family cannot be terminated or defeated. We are not only a force to reckon with, we *are* the force.

We stand, unified. Nothing and no one is between us. This is the reason why I was against Mo marrying Jacqueline Young. I am not prejudice, in the racial sense of the word – none of us are – it is just that no one meets the standards required to be a part of our household. We are a dynasty, one that cannot afford to be watered down by outsiders. I told Mo this, prior to his wedded affiliation with the Young family. Jacqueline's father is a commoner of sub-par intellect, who holds the notion that his race is the superior one. What he does not know is we are a far greater species than any other, whether white or black. We are rare breed without equal.

In my late teens, my father thought it time to introduce practice to enhance my ability to dominate opponents. My emotions and hormones were getting difficult to manage and he realized I needed assistance. Mo looked to me for guidance and answers to his questions about life and how it related to our beliefs. I could not be the example he required, if I was not in control of my own faculties. This began my journey into the teachings of Tantra.

Most people are accustomed with the term *tantric sex*; therefore they think that is the beginning and end of the practice. This is the mistake that most people make. They are close-minded and suffer tunnel vision. Our family belief is to maintain an open mind when it comes to learning. *We only know what we know*, my father says. We are great listeners because there is much insight to be gained in giving an ear to a person's thoughts. This is what makes us such great hunters, even my sisters. We can get into a person's psyche. The human ego asserts that one is deemed important, as others take interest in its ideologies. As it turns out, people will reveal and uncover things that would be left unsaid, under normal settings.

The power of Tantra keeps us cohesive and fluid as a unit; in a sense we are continual and unbroken. It is the backbone of our greatness, inherent. We live and breathe as one. We have a tantric lineage of skills learned, practiced, mastered and handed on with a special permission. It is uniquely ours, as we pull it into energy.

"Our belief is one radically different way of looking at, and acting in, the world around us. We do not give in to circumstances, we bend them to our will." My father spoke, to me, on the first day of our lesson.

"Tantra has an esoteric air about it, in that it is subliminal in nature. It responds under radar and threshold of daily awareness." He repeated, day after day.

"You cannot be impatient or unprepared, as you delve into this, otherwise it can be trouble for you." He warned.

I did not want to let my father down, so I suppressed my urges, until I was able to manage self-discipline. Yoga was crucial throughout transformation. Deep breathing techniques helped me put a yoke on my unruly nature, also linking me closer to my father, as my teacher and mentor. He was the epitome of self-control and he used his knowledge to train me.

"In order to be a better hunter or fighter, you will have to be a better thinker and better at concentrating." My father drilled.

I was ordered to sit and meditate for an hour each day, to find out what I wanted to do with my life and why. He told me to think why a hunter was necessary and how it benefits the family and me. It became clear, to me that I needed to protect the sanctity of our clan and all we hold dear. We are a close-knit group, vulnerable to absolutely no one, except to one another.

Mo stepped outside of our system when he met and married Jacqueline. She had a good head on her shoulders and a driving passion that she remained loyal to, in her career choice. Had she not been affiliated with ignorance and bigotry of her father, she would have been the perfect recruit. As it was, she had been indoctrinated in a way that she could not escape. She fought the mindset, yet the manifestation of her familial training, oozed out like liquid from cheesecloth. Jacqueline was not best fit for our dynamics.

All of us, in the Wells family, are practicing Tantra and yoga students. We are always learning and becoming more enlightened. There is never an end to coming into knowledge of oneself. My father says he is impressed with my level of commitment and how I will be able to teach the next generation. I am proud to have made such an impression on him. I have spent most of my life trying to please him, maintain his approval. He is a hard taskmaster, in some ways, and a loving patriarch when needed. I have never felt his disapproval, nor do I expect it. I strive for excellence in all he teaches. I listen, gleaning wisdom from the perfect example of his soul.

I followed my father's professional path. I excelled in school, never getting less than A's. I received a full academic scholarship to Massachusetts Institute of Technology, where I majored in the same field as my father, Civil Engineering, getting Bachelor's and Master's degrees. My course of study led me to geotechnical engineering. After 2, strenuous, licensing exams, I qualified to for the money that Parson Brinckerhoff is now paying me, right here in Norfolk, Virginia. I love the science in engineering, especially the material and environmental sciences. I also greatly enjoy geography and geology.

To most, that would qualify me a geek, of sorts, especially with the computer science expertise I possess. However, there is much more to Keyvaughn Wells, the man. I have spoken of the Tantra discipline and how my character has benefited from the practice. Yet, there is more. Some would call it a darker side. Cheyenne calls it my smoldering alter ego. I have been known to take a seat in the corner of my mind where I refuse to conform. Rage and villainous emotion reside there, remaining untouched by my efforts to corral that part of myself, and bring it to subjection of the yoke. The ire and venom appear to serve a purpose, within the family business, when I exercise undisciplined passions in order to protect the others. I certainly possess a secret enthrallment with peril and violence. There is an unhealthy association between that part of myself and the man I am, to most people. It is as if they feed off each other, making it a strange alliance of self.

Thinking of Cheyenne, I smiled. She is the most gifted and promising of the girls. She stands three inches taller than her sisters. Cheyenne's laughter brings warmth and happiness. Her skin is the color of caramel, contrasting my darker skin tone. Looking into her hazel eyes, I lose myself. She is my weakness; my kryptonite, as it was. I find pleasurable peace within the contours and curves of her body. I am intrigued with the flawlessness of her skin and its softness. She is beautiful and she becomes more attractive as her belly grows with our child, my son. Our love is very special and alive; it's palpable. No one could deny its power. We have been given the green light to explore every aspect of our dynamic affair. It goes to show just how bodhi we are. We accept what is, without looking to make sense of it. Love cannot be jailed by intelligence or philosophy. We are taken captive by its force.

In a couple of months, we would encounter Majestic Wells. Every time we call him, we will be speaking greatness into existence. His name will be who he is to become, superior to mundane issues, impressive, befitting a supreme ruler. He will be the beginning of my lineage within the family dynasty. I will teach him everything my father, his grandfather, taught me. He will be a pillar within the community, a brilliant man of honor and distinction.

I've seen Mo look at Cheyenne, admiring her gorgeous features, and her blossoming matrix. I know he is a tad envious of the seed growing within her. He spoke to Jacqueline of his desire to procreate, yet she maintained they needed more time to bond as a couple before bringing a life into the world. As he watched my woman beaming under the love and admiration of everyone, it caused him a little anguish. I would play the antagonist, stand behind her and rub her abdomen. She leaned into my body, wrapped her arms around my neck, and gyrated against my pelvis. I kissed her ear and whispered words only for her; my eyes never left my brother's face. I smiled as he smoldered at thought of his wife and her empty womb.

Walking in the precinct, torment was far from mind. I was in protective mode. We were closing ranks and tightening belts. There was to be no room for infringement from any force. We are one. As I walked through the door of the interrogation room and saw Mo sitting in the chair, shackled like a slave, I fought to retain disciplined equilibrium. There were two white officers both who looked mischievous and surly. Neither, of the two, smiled as I walked in with a lawyer. Instead, the taller one rushed from the other of the table. Then, I noticed a slight swell on my brother's lip.

"What the hell is going on in here?" My lawyer asked.

"We are questioning a murder suspect." The smaller cop answered.

"What are your names?" I demanded.

"I am Officer Mills and this is Officer Kent." The sneaky one responded.

"Well Officers Mills and Kent, I' Keyvaughn Wells and this is our attorney, Mr. Alan Getelman." I extended my hand to each of them, as did Alan.

"On what grounds do you hold my client?" Alan went right in.

"Your client was found at a murder scene with bloody clothes and bruised knuckles." I did not appreciate the tone in his voice.

"I ask you to do something about that accusatory tone in your voice, Officer." I noticed a wry grin cross Mo's lips.

"Listen Mr. Wells, like I told the suspect, it is not my tone that needs adjusting."

Alan cut in, "Let's not play which peacock has the more fanciful plumage. If there is no weapon involved or no confession, you have no grounds to keep Mr. Wells. Your evidence is circumstantial, at best. You did go into my client's home and the victim is his wife. So, if this is all you have, there is nothing more to be discussed."

Officers Mills and Kent stewed with their dilemma for a moment, before removing the handcuffs from Mo's wrists. He rubbed his wrists and tapped his feet a couple of times before stepping around the table.

"This is not the end. We'll get the evidence we need and we will be in touch with you, Mr. Wells." Officer Kent offered.

"As of this moment, there isn't a thing you can do to me, so save your threats for the next man."

"We know you had something to do with the murder, Morris. Believe me, when I tell you, you will be in this room again. Your fancy friend and overpaid lawyer will not be able to come and whisk you away, so easily." Kent spoke, again.

"I am more than a fancy friend, Officer Kent. I am his brother. If you approach my family, again, you will regret the day you were born." The knight bristled, within me.

Alan grabbed my arm in a silent plea. He motioned to leave the room. There was no reason to delay departure. I stepped aside, to allow Mo to depart. Alan was next. Before walking out of the door, I turned to the officers and said, "Don't doubt me."

When we reached the elevator, Alan took a call, leaving Mo and me alone. He looked sheepish, but in the dark about what was happening. I hated his lack of awareness to settings and circumstances. He would allow timidity to rise at most inopportune times. It left him vulnerable and open to attack more often than any of us liked. Our father left me to deal with weakness in my brother. There were occasions where I had to unleash uncontrolled sides, to train my brother. My words were scathing and toxic whenever Mo would come home feeling dejected by some comment or action of one of the students in his class. He didn't understand why everyone did not identify with his way. It angered me, so much, to where I reached a boiling point. He needed to be stronger, have thicker skin.

"What the hell is going on here?" I asked.

"I cannot recall, Keyvaughn. I remember locking my wife in the house, this morning and heading to work. The next thing that comes to mind is being hauled away by police, in handcuffs, and brought to the station." Mo looked perplexed.

"Jacqueline is dead."

"Yes, that is what I gather."

"What's up with bruises on your knuckles?"

"Jacqueline and I had a disagreement, last night, and I had to show her that I am in charge of our household." Mo answered.

"So, you hit your wife?" I shook my head.

"Yes. She needs to be reminded, from time to time, who wears the pants."

"Have you made a practice of striking your wife, Mo?" I could feel my ire rise.

"I have made a practice of reestablishing reins, whenever she thinks she can get out of line or be disrespectful." Mo looked me in the eyes.

"And that cannot be done, in a genteel way?" I returned his stare.

"Listen, don't you come telling me how to govern my own house. You didn't want to have anything to do with her, when I married her. What concern is it of yours how I choose to discipline my wife?" He squared his shoulders.

"I would not dare begin to advise you of your private affairs, unless it endangers us. A murder investigation could cause more trouble than you can handle. We have family to think of, at all times. We never act, independently, of that reality. No matter that you chose to go outside, you are responsible for protecting those who are your kin." I stepped closer.

"I didn't do anything." He didn't look or sound convinced.

"That is neither here nor there brother."

"How so?" He continued.

"Your wife is dead, Mo. The police have no suspect other than you. You are the person of interest. Her father will try to throw his religious clout around and add his bigotry to it. He will keep everyone looking in your direction. While they look at you, they will be looking at us." I pushed my forefinger into his chest.

Mo stepped away from my finger. "There is nothing to gain coming after me. I am innocent, Keyvaughn."

"How do you know?" I asked him, stepping closer. "How do you know you did not kill your wife, if you are telling me you have no recollection of going home? The police officers state, and you agree, they found you in the house with Jacqueline's body."

"Keyvaughn, I do not know the answers to those questions. I am confused. My wife is dead. I should be given some slack, at least from my family." Mo hissed through clenched teeth.

"Not having answers is not an option, in our alternate world. We need to be able to account for every moment of our day and night. We cannot afford a snafu to cause undue attention to us." I worked to devise a plan, some course of action. This news could be cataclysmic to us. We strive to stay under radar. We work in fields that keep a good portion of our money within legal confines of society. It's other streams of revenue that need protection from the prying eyes of the fraternal order of police.

"Don't you think I understand, Keyvaughn? I labor within the family business, just like the rest of you. I know the risks that come with having Big Brother peer into our lives. I have a meticulous record of excellent conduct, in the public." Mo was annoyed.

"I know you do." I conceded. "Alan will have his work cut out for him, with this one. They are not looking past you, bro. The whole penal system will work to bring down a successful black man."

"I don't know why one of us didn't become a lawyer. You spend a lot of your money to employ Mr. Getelman." Mo said.

"There isn't enough money in law, little brother. We are all about the Benjamins." I put my arm around his shoulder.

"True."

"Besides, we have to make the people, outside of our circle, think we need them for something, or they will use that as a reason to snoop." I pushed the button for the elevator, when I saw Alan head back in our direction.

"Well guys," Alan started. "We will have to hold a meeting with the family, soon. This can potentially be a very sticky situation for everyone, not just Morris, Jr."

That goes without saying, I said to myself. I did not want to think about it, right now. I glanced down at my wrist. I had enough time to make it to the obstetrician's office and meet Cheyenne for her appointment. I have not missed a meeting with her doctor since we found out the news. I did not want this to be the first time, either. She needed to know that I was fully committed to the whole process, pleasure to pain and all between.

"Well, I will be taking my leave." Alan said. "I have another meeting, if we are finished here." He looked from me to Mo.

I replied, "I imagine we have done all we can do, at the moment. Just remain at the ready, Alan. You know the system. They have retreated now, but the judicial wheels turn. They will be back, as they promise." *And, I will be ready to deal with them, when they do.*

CHEYENNE WELLS

I love my protruding belly. It provides me with a new sense of meaning in my life. A life is growing inside of me. This child is the product of an incredible love; one that transcends societal norms – it's ethereal. In my wildest dreams, I never would have imagined finding my soul's center in the manner in which it presented itself. Most people find my relationship narcissistic in nature. Yet, our paradigm works. We are lovers of us. Majestic, our son will add to the beauty that encircles us.

Keyvaughn is the most charismatic man, I have ever encountered. He has a certain 'je ne sais quoi' about him that draws me to him, even when I want to resist. There is a magnetism at all points. When he first approached me, I was appalled, at the idea. I could not fathom a relationship with him. He pursued and wooed me. He was patient, loving and kind. His advance was precise and full of purpose. He chose me. He would tell me I was more special than my sisters. He repeated it enough, setting up a belief system within my soul.

My heart began to rotate toward him and my body responded to his move. He would run his fingers through my hair and lure me in with his smoldering eyes. He would place his hand on my nape, lower his lips, and plant a kiss where his hands had been. I would feel goose bumps rise on my skin, as I became aroused. I trembled, and my breath caught. He knew he was wearing down my resolve. His tongue grazed my earlobe, ever so slightly, and I had the thrilling feeling of my uterus ballooning and causing a sensation to infuse my lower abdomen. He walked away, leaving me in heat. *He is teasing me and taunting my flesh*, I thought to myself.

A knock on my office door compelled me to cease my thought. I love going back to the first moment I realized my attraction to Keyvaughn. And, I was, more than a little, annoyed with the distraction. I wanted to fall into the flashback and let it play it out. Yet, I have a job to do. I glanced at the clock, as I rose from my desk. I smoothed my skirt over my hips and my shirt over my belly. *I love when Keyvaughn caresses my stomach and plants butterfly kisses on it, as he heads to my treasure box.* I felt myself shiver at the delicious nostalgia.

I opened the door, inviting my client to the office. I looked into the atrium of Dominion Counseling and Wellness Center. I enjoy working here. Everyone of us is successful. No one attempts to overpower the other, as we are secure in our field and area of expertise. Tamu Singletary is the visionary for this center. She has a doctorate degree in psychology and she works with patients who need medicine to control hormonal imbalances that disrupt mental acuity. At this stage of our growth, I, the inveterate psychologist, refer most of her patients.

I sat with my patient, listening to his murk and domestic dysfunction. He attributed his painful past to drug abuse and sexual addiction. He has not been involved in meaningful relationships, because he had imperious matriarchal figures. His mother and grandmother dominated the family. They ruled with iron hands. No one was able to step outside of stringent guidelines that had been put in place, by the Jezebel icons. I asked how he realized a correlation between the two. He said he needed a distraction from the domineering women, and it wasn't enough to run away, as their influence followed hard after him. His mind had been penetrated with their ceaseless onslaught of words and actions. So, he needed a distraction, and sex in all forms afforded him this outlet.

Near the end of the session, I asked him to ponder a question, "When a sex act ends, does the torment return? If so, wouldn't you be better off to find a solution that will have a longer lasting effect?"

I put my hand up to discourage him from answering the question, at this time. It required thought. I urged him to gauge his responses to his abuse and addictions. He agreed to the homework and rose to take his leave. I shook his hand, as I escorted him to the door. I looked at my watch and realized it was time to head to my ob/gyn appointment before I ran late.

I had not heard from Keyvaughn, since leaving home, this morning. I hoped he could get away to make it to the doctor's visit. I was grateful for his presence at any point, especially during this precious time.

I made a choice not to be a distraction during his day. He was so busy and he had much on his plate. I did not want to be the nagging partner. I love being his woman. I have blossomed under his adoration. He is the most attentive lover anyone can ask for...I am never left unsatisfied, yet I do long for more, as I am lulled to sleep at his experienced hand.

I felt elated, as I prepared to drive to the appointment. I wanted to see Keyvaughn's face. As the baby grew and I felt him move around, I imagined him mimicking his father. I adored him and this child he had given me. What an intimate expression of his love; allowing his seed to blossom within my body, letting the world know that I am his chosen one.

I headed out of the building, toward the parking lot and then I clicked the remote to unlock the door. As I stepped into the truck, my cell phone rang. I slipped in on the driver's side, dropped my purse on the passenger's seat, and then answered it.

"Hello."

"Hello, my sweet." Keyvaughn's voice filled my space.

"Keyvaughn, I did not expect to hear from you, once the midmorning break passed. What a pleasant surprise." I was thrilled, as I started the car.

"I know. I missed you and I will be a few moments late. I had an emergency that took me away from work, until now." His voice was apologetic.

"I appreciate your thoughtfulness. I will alert the receptionist, so that you can be escorted to the room, if I have been called to the back by the time you get there."

"I will do my best to get there before then. I do not want you to go back there, alone. There was a situation with Mo. I will tell you later. I do not want to concern you with it." His voice soothed and calmed me in a way nothing else could.

"I will wait for you."

"Good. I love you, Cheyenne."

"I love you, too, Keyvaughn."

We disconnected and my smile would not fade away. I was thrilled to hear from Keyvaughn. I hope the emergency was not too much of a problem. He hated stress. He wanted to avoid it, at all costs.

I started the car, backed out of the parking space and headed for my appointment. I took my time, as the roads were like an ice-skating rink, due to inclement weather. My smile broadened, as I thought about Keyvaughn purchasing this Navigator for me. He did not want me to be concerned about bad weather and traction issues with a smaller car. This vehicle is so luxurious. It's a beast on gas, particularly with the rising cost of fuel these days. It is of no concern of mine; my man foots the bill to fill up the tank. I am well taken care of and very spoiled. I don't know how people deal with me, at times.

I am lavished with more expensive gifts and attention than any woman deserves. I do not have to lift a finger to do anything, if I choose not to bother. Even with his busy schedule, my man cooks for me and brings my food to the table. He cleans up after me, does my laundry and bathes me, every day. I get a warm oil massage, before I go to bed, and he makes love to me before I head out to work. He pays for my manicures, pedicures and for me to get my hair done. My money is for me to do with as I wish.

I pressed the brake, as I noticed a fender bender in front of me. Many people were rubbernecking and traffic came to a halt. I checked the clock on the dashboard. I had no worries with time. It would be great if folks understood there is no need to rush, if time is allotted for mishaps and minor inconveniences. I am sure the drivers, in the accident, would have benefited from this mindset. Perhaps they would not be in the predicament they were in, had they allowed themselves more time.

I felt Majestic squirming, in tight quarters. So, I placed my hand on my abdomen and wondered at the splendor of pregnancy. I know every experience is not the same, yet there is much to be thankful for. We have been graced to be the sex selected to bear mankind in our bodies. We are the recipients of seed, and hopefully planted in love. We sprout and blossom as our child grows from our tender care and nurturing. Sure, there is work to be done if we are to regain shape, but it's worth it. A beautiful baby springs forth, from our womb, and we are adored because of it.

A warm flush infused me as I recalled the moment of our son's conception. It was the most outstanding session Keyvaughn and I had together. We are so superior together. Foreplay began hours before we made love. A kiss planted, here. A caress felt, there. Soft words spoken in my ear, every chance he got. He pulled me to his lap, we watched television, and he gently stroked my hair. I felt his manhood against my buttocks. I was highly aroused by the time he called me to bed. I was aching for him to work his magic. He would take me to the edge, and then pull back. My heart pounded, wildly, and he urged me to take deep, cleansing breaths. He put butterfly kisses on all erogenous zones. As he lightly touched my skin, I burned with longing. I needed to feel him, swollen and sizeable, inside of me. He obliged me and I felt his heat fill me up and take me over the top, again and again and again.

I felt myself getting moist at the reverie. I needed to free my mind, before I arrived at the obstetrician's office. I was scheduled for an internal exam, to check for effacing and dilation. It would be so embarrassing to be turned on while the doctor was doing her job. I looked out of the driver's side window, as I passed the police officers and the tow truck that had been called to the scene. I noticed a woman standing on the median looking shaken. One of the cops was speaking with her and she nodded her head, as the tears fell down her cheeks. I imagined the tears felt like shards of glass on her cold face. She didn't have on a coat and that was odd. It was below freezing, since yesterday morning. I wondered why she would not have put a jacket on, in this weather. In that moment, she walked over to her vehicle and grabbed it.

My phone rang. I wondered if Keyvaughn was calling me back advising he would not make the visit. I clicked the 'talk' button and greeted my caller. It was my mother, checking on me.

"Cheyenne, I just wanted to see how you were getting along on these icy roadways." She sounded concerned.

"Mommy, I am well. This Navigator has no trouble on ice or snowfall. I passed an accident, a few moments ago."

"I hope everyone is alright."

"Yes, it was a minor fender bender. I was thinking, people should allow themselves more time to get to their destinations. I assume the incident was caused because someone was speeding or rushing to get from one place to the other."

"Well, take your time, young lady. I do not want anything to happen to you or my grandbaby." I could hear the smile, in her voice, as she spoke of the baby.

"I am doing everything, within my power, to ensure Majestic stays safe. I can't wait to see his little face."

"Don't be anxious, dear. Let him cook until he is ready. We want him healthy and also ready to face the world."

"Yes,. You're right. Besides, I should savor these moments when it is just he and I. Once he is born, I will have to share him with family." I put my hand on my belly.

"Oh yes, you will! I am going to be first, in line, to hold him the moment he is born."

"First in line, after Keyvaughn, of course. He is biting at the bit, himself." I laughed.

"Of course." My mother laughed, too.

"Well, let me get off of the phone. I am turning into the medical center's parking lot. I love you, Mommy. I will call, once the appointment is over."

"See ya, Cheyenne. Call my cell phone, as I am out of the office today." My mother hung up, quickly.

I drove around for a few, before I found a parking space close to the entrance. I pulled into the space, turned off the ignition and sat back, enjoying the warmth of the truck. I reached into my bag to retrieve my flat shoes for walking on ice. I dropped them, on the floor, in front of me so I could slip them on. It was becoming increasingly difficult to bend over, these days. Keyvaughn helped with my shoes, when I prepared for work.

I noticed a shadow, of a person, on the passenger side of the car. I was startled, at first. Then, I realized it was Keyvaughn. He climbed into the truck and leaned over to kiss me, passionately, on the lips. I dropped my bag and wrapped my arms around his neck, as he moved closer to me. I closed my eyes, as I felt his tongue gently probing my mouth. I felt my nipples harden and my vagina began to pulsate. He ran his hands through my hair and I sighed. He broke the embrace. I noticed the desire, in his eyes. I am sure; he saw that he was not alone.

"Hey baby." He said, huskily.

"Hey, yourself."

I sat back, in the seat. I needed to catch my breath. He never failed to take me to this place, when he kissed me with such ardor. I cannot resist him. I have stopped trying. I welcome his attention and his passion. Keyvaughn got out of the truck and walked around to the driver's side. He opened my door and lifted me out of the vehicle. He slipped his hands into my coat and pulled me to himself. I pressed my breasts to his chest, as he caressed my bottom. Majestic squirmed. I wondered if he knew that his father was near.

"Do you feel your son, Keyvaughn?"

"Yes." He moved his hand to my belly and rubbed, tenderly. He bent and kissed it.

I noticed onlookers slow down to witness our exchange. Smiles crossed the women's faces, at the attention Keyvaughn was lavishing on me. They must feel a twinge of jealousy, as they enter the building alone. I am sure every lady would simply love for the father of her youngster to accompany them to their appointments. I understood, in that moment, how lucky I was to have such an adoring man.

Keyvaughn closed the door, behind me, after he retrieved my bag and cell phone. He took my hand and we walked toward the entrance, together. He opened the door and allowed me to walk in, telling me to wait for him to get the second door. We entered the building and headed toward the bay of elevators. I pushed the button, to summon the lift, and we waited. I put my arm around my man's waist and leaned into him, feeling his warmth.

"I was pleasantly surprised to see you, just arriving." Keyvaughn stated.

"Yes. I was delayed by a fender bender. I am thankful for it, now." I smile. "If it hadn't been for the accident, I would not have received such a superb greeting." I reached up to kiss him.

We walked into the elevator with two other women. They were pregnant, as well. One looked further along than I was and I felt slightly envious. She did not have long to wait. I remembered what my mother said, when I was on my way here. I quelled the covetousness, and breathed a sigh of joy, as Keyvaughn softly kissed my temple.

"Your day will come, soon enough, baby."

We arrived on the eighth floor and all of us departed the elevator and headed toward the office. Keyvaughn held the door for all of the women, before he stepped inside. I signed in, at the front desk, and he took care of the co-pay. We took a seat, in the waiting area and grabbed a magazine to bide the time. I flipped through the pages, absentmindedly. I wanted to be in a place where I could show my man how much I loved him. I had to redirect my thoughts, again. I needed to change my panty liner, after the check-up. *Perhaps, I should dry off prior to the visit*, I thought.

"I will be right back, sweetie."

"Are you alright?" Keyvaughn questioned.

"I need to take care of something, in the bathroom. You started something that I do not want the doctor to be privy to, when she examines me." I kissed him.

"I can come with you and take care of that for you." He spoke, seductively.

"Oh, I know you can." I answered. "Later."

"You best believe it." He smiled.

I walked away, knowing he watched my behind. I moved my hips, in an inflated fashion, to tease him. I opened the door to the bathroom and let it close behind me. I headed to a stall. I heard some panting, in the stall, beside me. It sounded like the breathing we learned in Lamaze class.

"Everything okay, over there?" I asked.

"I'm in labor." Her answer was rushed. "I feel like I need to push and I am afraid." I could hear her soft sobs, between all of the heavy breathing.

"I will go and get some help."

"Please, don't leave me!" She sounded a bit hysterical. "The baby is coming. I can feel her head."

"Is the stall door open?"

I heard a latch being clicked, and I opened the door. I saw the woman, sitting on the commode, sweat beaded on her forehead. She was panting, as she held on to the sides of the toilet. She had on a skirt, which was a good thing. At least her pants did not have to be taken off, if the baby was near.

"You really should have a doctor, in here."

"Don't you think I know that, Miss!" She yelled, and then she quickly apologized. "Forgive me."

"No need to apologize. I understand. The situation is tense."

She reached out to grab my hand and she squeezed. I walk into the stall, with her.

"Can you look? I am afraid." She looked me in the eyes. I could see her fear.

I bent, at the knees, and peered between her legs. I gasped. She was right! I could see the baby looking right, at me. I stood up, quickly.

"Ma'am, the baby's head is out. I am going to have to grab hold of her, so she will not fall into the toilet." I placed my hands under her bottom. She pushed a couple of times and a baby girl fell into my hands. I placed the girl in her mother's arms.

My cell phone rang; I used the bathroom tissue to wipe the blood from my hands. It was Keyvaughn concerned I was taking so long. I informed him what happened and asked him to alert the front desk, so they could send a doctor. He hung up, quickly, as I redirected my attention to the woman who had just given birth in the bathroom.

"Thank you, so much..."

"Cheyenne." I replied to a silent question.

"Thank you Cheyenne," her smile widened by her beautiful gift. "My name is Mitrice Reynolds. You are a godsend." Tears filled her eyes.

"You are welcome, Mitrice. I am glad that I happened into the restroom. I would be terrified if it had been me."

"I am too."

I left to get some paper towels and dab her brow. Just then, two doctors entered the bathroom and headed toward the stall. I stepped aside to give them clear access. I glanced at the door and saw Keyvaughn looking anxious.

"Are you alright, Mitrice?" I asked.

"Yes, thanks Cheyenne. God bless you."

I smiled and walked to Keyvaughn. I don't get my blessings from God, I thought, as I took my seat. Everything I get comes from my family. We work hard to get things we want. We are established with high paying jobs and our family business tops off the rest. I do not need a god to bless me. We are doing fine, without god. We are gods.

PATRICIA WELLS

I love my family. I am like a lioness when it comes to protecting my children. My husband, Morris, and I, have raised a great group. They are successful and excel in their fields of choice. They use their line of work to help build the family business. What more can a mother want? I smiled, as I drove the highway. My life was good.

I married the love of my life, Morris Wells, Sr. I met him, while I interned in Bolivia, studying for a degree in biology. I traveled with a research team of ethno botanists, into posterior regions of Bolivia, searching for traditional elders. We neared a woman, on a porch, smoking marijuana. Her name is Milandrous Samba Wells. She was the eldest female in the village. As we neared her, I felt as if we entered a time warp. I could feel the ages pass and immediately I was transported into her era. I could sense her feeling of pride as the team chose her family to help with our investigation into the use of the plants native to her land.

I learned much about the land and history from Milandrous. The researchers stayed in

Bolivia for the entire summer. She took me under her wing and she taught me what she knew about indigenous plants. I am sure it helped that her grandson and I were got close, during my tenure in the country. She told me that although much of southern Altiplano is saline and barren, there is a coarse bunchgrass, called ichu, common in the north. It is used, mainly to feed llamas. A tough wind-resistant shrub, called tola, and moss-like cushions called yareta are widely used for fuel, along with cactus shrub. Then there are totara reeds, used for thatching, feeding livestock, and Indian boats called balsas. I furrowed my brow, when she used the term thatching, and she kindly informed me that it is much like straw and it is used as a covering for roofs and grain stacks. As I researched further, I found that it is dead grass that is bound with leaves, stems and roots that build up along the base of living grass of a lawn. We use it as ground cover around the flowerbeds at the Blackwater Ecological Preserve, and the botanical gardens at Old Dominion University where I am currently a Professor of Botany in the Department of Biological Sciences.

Milandrous and her family are what the natives call Afro Bolivians (Bolivians with African origin). Her lineage is from Africans enslaved by Spanish Conquistadors who needed help mining silver in Cerro Rico, Rich Mountains in Bolivia, after the natives became too ill to do the work on their own. It was required that blacks (Africans) and the browns (natives) work together in the mines for twelve hours a day, once they reached age 18. They had been known to put children to work, too. The miners were exposed to asbestos, toxic gases, cave-ins and explosions; few survived more than 6 months.

Spaniards' way of fortifying slaves was to have them chew on the leaves from the coca plant. Milandrous leaned down to pick up a basket, containing leaves. She held it up, as she told me it has become a very important element in the Bolivian culture. The plant is an agricultural plant consumed by Bolivians; however, it can be processed into cocaine. Whenever the slaves chewed the leaf, it numbed their senses to cold, staved off feelings of hunger and alleviated altitude sickness. This enabled slaves to work longer without taking needed breaks. She broke piece off, offered it to me, after placing a piece in her mouth. She told me to chew. I was in no position to decline. I noticed she was not actually chewing, but sucking the leaf. I followed suit. She went on to inform me that the veins, of the leaf, had been stripped to avoid the devastating effects of hard elements on the lining of the mouth. I was not to swallow, nor was I to fully macerate the leaf, just "mush" it enough to break the cell membranes and allow them to dissolve slowly in my saliva.

After 15 or 20 minutes, she offered me a lilijta, comprised of herbaceous ashes from the quinoa and plantain. I, later, found out this was used as an alkaline medium to maximize the action from the leaf. Soon, I felt the aesthetic effects on the inside of my mouth, tongue and throat. Milandrous told me the Andean custom of chewing the coca or making a coca infusion was used to treat ailments (i.e. headaches, toothaches, cramps, and more) and help alleviate pain. I broke my finger, while on an expedition; a poultice was, made with coca leaf, and applied to the break. I must say, it helped.

I noticed I had a feeling of exhilaration and I needed to busy myself. I was less tired and a sense of euphoria surrounded my head. Morris and I would chew coca leaf, then head to a secluded area behind the house to make love. It was an intense rush of stimuli and the orgasms were out of this world. I remember asking him how many girls he seduced with the magical effects of the coca plant? He assured me he had not been with any girl, which I found hard to believe with the skill he seemed to possess as he handled my body.

As our research went forward, Milandrous continued to advise that the Conquistadors noticed a considerable increase of capacity and yield when the effects of the coca leaf enhanced miners' work, improving their staying power. Blacks and browns were known to chew leaf 3 or 4 times per day, depending on workload. I asked whether it was habit forming or produced undesirable affects, if they discontinued the practice. She assured me there were no withdrawal symptoms when the practice was not being utilized. It was not uncommon for a miner to abandon practice when work was light or nonexistent. She said if anyone stated they were addicted to coca leaf or cocaine, there had to be another additive that made this true, like injecting it into the veins.

Another plant that has been used to help with erectile dysfunction is the maca root. It is used to make revitalizing candies and syrups that can be given to the men as a natural remedy for their ailment.

As coca leaf and maca root are organic, these medicines are metabolized and the body assimilates them more easily. There were no Indians or Afro Bolivians dealing with adverse reactions caused by use of indigenous plants. Milandrous assured me she and her family had been using these, and several plant barks, treating malaria attacks and other conditions.

What I learned was of great importance in my passion to become an ethno botanist. I made several trips to Bolivia, with research teams, and we became educated in the correlation amid plants, black magic and religious rites. The Samba Wells' were of a group called the Kallawayas, conventional shamans of Bolivia. Their blend of super natural and knowledge has tapped into the healing powers Mother Nature has to offer to those who avail themselves to it. They are noted healers, in the region and, they were invited into the inner royal sanctum where they learned their sacred language. This dialect is known only to Kallawayan people and is used when discussing private and sacred matters. Milandrous did not disclose this information to me.

When I visited Bolivia for undergraduate and graduate study, Morris and I resumed our relationship. We were in love and our auras constantly drew to one another. It was as if he used his family's black magic on me, because I felt him while I slept in the United States. We were kindred souls and there was no denying that fact. On my last trip to Bolivia, Morris advised that he would return to Virginia with me. He would continue study in Civil Engineering and find work on stateside.

When we arrived in the Commonwealth, Morris got an apartment and I moved in with him. My parents were appalled at the blackness of his skin. I told my parents I could not believe they chose racism within a race. My father advised that Morris was not a black man who could call himself an African American. I was astonished at the tomfoolery of it all. I asked the difference between an Afro Bolivian and the blacks of the United States? We are from African decent, I retorted. Our ancestors were slaves. The only distinction comes into play as it pertains to where slave boats took our forefathers. He continued to snub his nose, until I declared my love for Morris and intent on becoming his wife. My family has grown to love my black man like he was their own; at least that is how they acted when we were around.

I had gotten so wrapped up and consumed with my reverie that I missed my exit on the highway and had to double back, to reach my destination. I was going to meet with my daughters, Olivia and Sahara, to plan the baby shower for Cheyenne. They wanted to have lunch at Eaton Gogh on Harrington Avenue, in Norfolk. I looked forward to she-crab soup, salad, sandwich and slice of chocolate cake. I turned off of Hampton Boulevard and headed east on Harrington to the restaurant. As I turned into the parking lot, I noticed Olivia's car and an open space beside it. I pulled into the space, turned off the ignition, grabbed my purse from the passenger's seat, and then opened the door. I tested my footing prior to exiting the car, to ensure I would not slip. The owners had done a good job sanding the asphalt to prevent falls.

I walked to the eatery and took a cursory look about the place. I noticed Olivia and Sahara seated at a booth, with menus in hands. Sahara waved to me. The two sat on one side of the booth, leaving me to sit opposite them. I needed room for my hips and buttocks. I smiled, to myself, as a thought crossed my mind. Morris loves my body measurements, no matter how they have risen in our 35 years of marriage. At one point, I was so self-conscious about the increased inches. I would not shower with my husband or take my clothes off in his presence. This angered him. He stated he felt judged. I was amazed. How could I be judging him when I felt like he would criticize my larger frame? He looked me in the eyes, and said I passed sentence on him by attributing something to his charge that he was never given the opportunity to debate. Since then, I never hid from him and he never looked at me with a critical eye. He has exemplified unconditional love to me, in a way no one else has.

"Hello, my darling daughters."

"Hello, Mommy." They replied in unison.

"I see you have already perused the menu, so we should be ready to place our orders. I know what I want." I removed my jacket and settled into the cushioned bench.

"I have been looking at she crab soup." Olivia said. "They have French onion soup, on the menu, today. I may try that."

"I will forfeit soup, today." Sahara joined in. "I am feeling the salad and sandwich combo they offer."

"I have a chill in my bones so I will have she crab soup." I added.

Before the waiter returned with our order, we discussed the shower. We planned on the color scheme of navy blue and white, which was a combination of Cheyenne and Keyvaughn's favorite colors. It would be perfect colors for Majestic, rich and pure. There would be very little guests, as most do not understand the special dynamic of their relationship. Too many times, those outside of the circle have spoken of the old wives tale of it being taboo and frowned upon. When enemies chose to voice their opinion, I chose to tell them to take their critical asses and go straight to hell. No one had the right to judge what cannot be contained. We are not responsible for the choices of the heart. If Morris and I do not take offence to it, then no one can. I am honored Keyvaughn chose Cheyenne. I don't have to explain to anyone. None of us have to explain what we do.

When food arrived, we put chat on hold to savor the dishes. We were delighted with soups, salads, sandwiches and desserts. Even the lemonade and sparkling apple cider tasted especially delicious. We asked for boxes and plated up what we could not eat. I wanted to share my chocolate cake with Morris, when he got home. I love watching decadent delicacies enter Morris's mouth, including myself.

I put a charge card on the placard and handed it to the waiter. The girls doubled the tip, placing it under a ketchup bottle, on the table. I returned the card to my wallet, once the waiter was finished with it. We gathered our purses, doggie bags and coats before leaving the Eaton Gogh. I kissed my babies and we headed to our cars. I bundled my fur collar around my neck, to ward off the blast of arctic air that came off the Chesapeake. I clicked the button, on the keyless remote, so the car would be unlocked and turned on when I got to it. I stepped in, quickly closing the door. The temperature was set to a perfect 72 degrees and I basked in the comfort of its warmth. I sighed and closed my eyes. I never missed opportunity to relish in the things that bring me joy.

After a long moment, I adjusted myself in the seat, fastened the seatbelt securely in place and slid the transmission to reverse. I glanced at the rearview mirror to ensure my safe departure from the space. My cell phone rang. I moved onto Harrington, and stopped at the traffic light. I answered the call. It was Morris.

"Hello, sweetheart."

"Hello, beautiful bride." His Spanish accent caressed my eardrum.

"Morris, I love you." I could not help it.

"Te quiero, cariño. ¿Cómo estás?" I loved it when he spoke in his native tongue.

"I am doing well, my dear. The girls and I shared lunch and we also made plans for Cheyenne's baby shower. We ate at Eaton Gogh, on Harrington Avenue. And, I have a surprise for your mouth."

"Es lo que?" He taunted me with seductive words.

"It can be me, if that is what you want. However, I was referring to a dessert, one made in the kitchen of the restaurant, not in secret workings of my mother's womb." I smiled, to myself.

"¿Qué tienes para mi?" He asked.

"It is chocolate cake, if you must know. Why do you never let me surprise you?" I checked my side mirrors, preparing for my turn onto Hampton Boulevard.

"I love chocolate." His voice was smooth.

"So do I." I could play the game, too.

"I would love to continue foreplay; there will be time for that. I have a purpose for the call." His tone grew serious.

"Ok. I am listening." I made a left turn and checked my speed.

"Keyvaughn called to advise Jacqueline has been killed and Morris, Jr. was taken in for questioning."

"Oh my goodness, Morris!" I exclaimed.

"Yes, this is not the best news we could hear, however, Alan was summoned and he got Morris released." I heard the keys on his laptop click, in the background.

"What does this mean for us?"

"It means we need to continue with our planned course. We are deliberately careful and we have been aboveboard, within the confines of the law. There is no reason for us to be concerned. Cheyenne may need to curtail her department, for now, as it may be the first visible to the judicial all Seeing Eye." He made his statements, in a matter of fact tone.

I centered myself and relaxed, listening to my husband's voice. He did not appear worried neither anxious; therefore, there was no cause for alarm, on my part. I loved his ability to calm my raging seas. I could be a bit high strung when it came to my family and our welfare. I would never have made it, in our line of business, had it not been for the peacefulness of my chocolate king. He ruled our dynasty with finesse. He possessed an amazing sense of savoir-faire. He would handle his business, if need be, yet we never feared him. He was sovereign in our household. Supreme headship belonged to him and we adored him, in his role. Morris is the man of my dreams; better still, he surpassed my wildest dreams. I could never imagine a more powerful, yet tender man, if I had created him myself.

"Ok. We are good. We are not threatened, right?" I asked one more question.

"I will never allow anything or anyone to come near us. They may try, but I will come down on them with such wrath and vengeance that will spread throughout their entire affiliation. I will leave nothing untouched. They will be obliterated." The danger and violence, in his voice, turned me on. His words were deliberate and full of intent.

"I know you will, sweetie. And for that and a host of other reasons, I love you."

"You are my whole universe, Patricia, and the children are an extension of you. We are good." His words were weighty.

"I will have more than the chocolate cake waiting for you, when you get home. Be sure to come straight to the bedroom and lock the door behind you." I smiled.

"*Estoy listo*. I am ready for you now."

"I am headed home, as we speak. You can come when you are prepared; and I mean that in every sense of the word." I teased.

"Never before you, darling." He asserted.

"One of the many reasons for my undying affinity to you and all you are."

"I know it." He laughed. "I recall coca leaf enhanced moments in Bolivia behind my *abuela's* house. Your excitement amazed me and drove me to think of new ways to enhance upon it."

"All of your creations are masterpieces. You will not be duplicated. You possessed me. I think I still am possessed."

"There is more where that came from. You keep me on my toes." He laughed.

"And you keep mine curled." I stated.

"I will hurry home and sate that appetite. Let me finish up here, and tie these loose ends, at the office. I want you naked, a beautiful plate for that chocolate cake."

We disconnected the line and I continued home, with a smile on my face.

MORRIS WELLS, SR.

My *abuela* and *abuelo* instilled in me the qualities to make me the man I am, today. I am strong and deliberate. I am a fierce warrior and hunter. I am an assassin and I trained my sons to be the same. We take no prisoners, to protect those we love. We are fierce lovers of ourselves. It may be African blood coursing through my veins or the Bolivian Indian life force under which I was trained. It doesn't matter from where it derives. What matters is that I possess what it takes to get what I want. I am fearless, except when it comes to losing what I have built to provide for my family. I will do what is necessary to keep the lifestyle we are accustomed to.

While in Bolivia, *mi familia* was strong and influential. We were given great power by the heads of state and other royal factions. We possessed means to make the world disappear and pain abate. As the village healers of shaman lineage, we knew what was needed, no matter the ailment. My *abuela* was well respected; revered, by the powers that be and the other villagers. She could summon up spirits that would haunt souls, with smoke of an indigenous plant. Fear begat honor and our status grew.

I was engrafted to royal ranks and also afforded opportunity to get my education, in civil engineering. The country paid for tuition and housing. They paid my *abuela* and *abuelo* for me to learn at university. I gleaned all I could, until it was time to move on and start my own dynasty. *Mi familia* did not hinder me or compel me to stay in Bolivia. They wanted more for me, and so did I. *Abuela* noticed a beautiful mocha skinned angel, named Patricia, had besotted me. She was a research analyst with a team of ethno botanists that wanted to learn secrets of *mi familia's* heritage.

I imagined she would be uninterested in someone with skin as dark as blackstrap molasses. Americans tended to look at my skin tone, with disdain. It was as if they rejected their African roots, showing bias to dark skinned people. However, that was not the case with Patricia Wells. She was stunning, and her intellect aroused me. I would listen to her voice and her choice of verbiage, as she conversed with *abuela*. I would rub my hardened member, on the other side of the door. I had no experience with women; but my *abuelo* instructed me on the ways to please them. I wanted to use these skills to please this creature that had come to my land, in search of our rich knowledge and heritage.

I was home, from university, when Patricia visited with *abuela*. I took her hand, in greeting, and kissed it. I saw the *la piel de gallina* rise on her arm. I looked into her light brown eyes and unveiled me to her. I bared my soul, in the exchange; I could see into hers, as well. We connected on a subconscious level. I knew I would have her before sunset. I prepared myself, while they spoke of the land and plants were used for medicinal purposes. They talked, further, about revitalizing effects of coca leaf when chewed or sucked. I looked out of the window and I saw her heightened awareness. It was when I developed the idea to use coca leaf in our lovemaking.

As the day waned, *abuela* took her leave for her evening nap. It was the time to sweep her off her feet. I prided myself in intellectual prowess. I would entertain a talk with Patricia and seduce her, as she had done me. I walked onto the porch and sat next to her. I placed my hand upon her hand and she turned to question me, yet she did not draw back or push me away. I spoke to her, in native tongue. She was fluent, in Spanish; she understood every word. Her eyes softened and her fingers intertwined with mine. I moved closer and leaned in to kiss her dew softened lips. My tongue, tenderly, explored her mouth. I placed my other hand on the nape of her neck as her head fell back, slightly. This gave more access to her delicious mouth. I craved more.

I jumped off the porch and lifted her to the ground, leading her around to the back of the house. There was a clearing, deep in the forest, where I had already placed a blanket and some coca leaves in a basket. My arm wrapped around her small waist and rested on the round top of her *trasero.* We stopped, often, before reaching our destination. I kissed her mouth and then caressed her skin. I lifted the bottom of her skirt to feel the softness of her thighs. I heard her moan, as I planted kisses on her neck, shoulders and soft mounds of her breasts. I wanted to taste all of her.

When we arrived at the set place, I looked into her eyes to see if I saw a look of appall. I saw nothing of the sort. Instead, I saw a passion I could not have dreamed. She wanted me, as much as I wanted her. She removed her shirt, exposing her naked breasts. She was notwearing a brassiere. I placed my hands around her waist and rested them at the small of her back, as I drew her into me. My mouth, hungry for her breasts, suckled gently. I flicked my tongue across one nipple, as my finger caressed the other one. Her breaths were coming rapid. I removed my mouth from her bosom, to speak into her ear.

"*Respirar. Inspirar.*" I told her to breathe in and to breathe out. "*Despacio.* Slowly."

Patricia's breathing regulated. I kissed an earlobe, then behind her ear.

"*No se olvide.*" I encouraged her to never forget.

"I won't, Morris." She promised.

"*Bueno.*" I stroked her back, shoulders and waist. Her hips gyrated.

She began to unbutton my shirt and slide it off of my shoulders. She kissed my chest and ran her fingers down the length of my back. Her hands reached down to unfasten my pants, as I slipped her skirt off of her hips. Both fell to the ground, as I laid her down. She had on no panties. I could smell her desire, and my ardor was stoked. My member was throbbing, yet I maintained control. I heard my *abuelo's* voice, in my head, *nunca pervert el control*.

My mouth and tongue traced a path to her treasure. Her back arched to meet my tongue, as I tasted of her nectar. I was intoxicated with cloying liquid that flowed freely from her. I fondled her breasts, as I feasted on her. She smelled amazing. My olfactory nerves were seared. I was locked and honed in. I swirled my tongue around and around. I dipped it inside of her and traced the path from her *ano* to vagina. Her body began to quiver and I knew her time was close. I put my hands on her buttocks and pulled her closer. I did not want to miss a drop of sweet ambrosia. She climaxed while her body quivered and bucked with intensity. She was ready.

That moment, I knew she would be mine. I had been ruined for other women and I did not care. I knew I needed to finish out my term, at the university, before I would be able to contemplate future plans. Patricia assured me she would return, the following summer and asked would I wait for her. I promised I would. I had no choice. She looked, at me, with a question in her eyes.

"*Me pregunta.*" I gave her permission to ask me what she wanted.

"How many women have you brought to this place and plied with the stimulant that one feels with the coca leaf?"

"You are the first."

"How can that be, Morris?" Tears were in her eyes. "You have done things to me I could never have dreamed. You possessed me, like an expert lover."

"You are the only one. *Mi abuelo* trained me for this. From the look and sound of it, he has done well." I smiled, hoping to see her radiance returned. I was not let down.

"You spoiled me, Morris." She whispered.

I kissed her trembling lips and fire raged.

This passion is what has driven our lives. We've been loyal to one another, fiercely loyal, at times. We have shown our fangs, on more than one occasion. We do not take to anyone who seeks to disturb the balance of our kingdom. We defend it, at all cost. We trained our children to do the same. Our ranks will never be broken, no matter our link with the outside world. We are closely knit, and inseparable.

This is stance we took, to defend Morris, Jr. We must ward off any attackers that seek to drag him through mud. I thought I was going to have to take out Kenneth Young, when Morris, Jr. got involved with his daughter, Jacqueline. His bigotry was unruly and he overstepped his boundaries. He walked around with his nose in the air, as if he had a right to look down on us. He is nothing, to me. He was insignificant. He emitted religious anecdotes, thinking they had power to overtake us. We were much stronger than his false sense of faith. We had more loyalty to one another than he to the god he served. He was a hypocrite, to the 100th degree. Still, he assumed an elitist pose. My youngest son outranked him in intelligence and alliance. He did a great favor, by leaving his daughter's life.

With this set of circumstances, he will work to superimpose himself into our world. He has religious clout. His parishioners and advocates have more power than he does, as they stand in agreement. If they feel he was wronged or demeaned, they will latch on to the cause and wrangle it to ground. We would assess the atmosphere and see where we could cut them off at the knees. We are no fools. We understand we cannot obliterate an entire community; however, we could diffuse them, by getting rid of selected leaders of the battalion.

When I spoke with Keyvaughn and Alan, earlier, I was assured they would take the frontline with this assault. I would cover backends, keeping Morris, Jr. intact and ready. He had propensity to fall out of rank when he felt threatened. He was prone to anxiety attacks and falling into a fugue state. This has not boded well for us, in the past, as it left much to be cleaned up in the aftermath. He would suffer from complete amnesia during a fugue episode; we would be searching around, blindly. I am sure there was 'overkill' in some times, but we could never be too meticulous. Keyvaughn advised this was such incident.

Morris, Jr. had no recollection of the time period between leaving for work and being taken into custody. Police officers found him at the home, with bruised hands and bloody clothes. There were no witnesses; circumstantial evidence could be explained away, it would appear that Morris, Jr. was in the clear. Yet, the law was a sticky trap, when it came to the matter of a black man and crime against their white counterparts. Again, unknowns were everywhere. This was where I came in. I would mastermind the cleanup effort, if there arose a need for it. I would decide who to handle and how.

I would handle Morris, Jr. later. My time was better-spent making love to my wife. I finished up at the office and shut down my laptop. I summoned my secretary and I asked if there was anything I may have missed. Once she checked the calendar and her to-do list, she told me I had a green light to leave, for the day. I, in turn, gave her a nod to take the rest of the day off. We turned off lights, after removing trash from bins and placing bags in the hallway. We walked out to elevators and took a ride to the parking garage. I bid her farewell. I climbed into my Infiniti truck, started the ignition and turned on the CD player. I enjoyed jazz. The soulful sounds of the saxophone filled the interior of the truck, as I pulled out of the parking space.

I thought about Cheyenne's appointment. We were excited about the new member, little Majestic. I hoped she got a glowing report from the doctor. I would be sure to ask her, once I had my fill of my wife. I loved making love with her, after a long day at the office. My mind hones in and focused on one thing that mattered to me, in this world. I was consumed by passion and her love. It drove me. I needed to feel her underneath me. I loved her body. It is shaped perfectly. I remember her having a moment with body image issues. She hid herself and deprived me of pleasure. We had a heated talk about it; it was resolved and we are on course.

I turned on a signal, as I prepared to make a left turn. My mind was clearing and I was prepared for the session. I knew there were other matters, yet they would have to wait. I needed to connect with my wife. Regroup. Refocus, and then I would be able to deal with other matters. I checked my mirror. I was most comfortable, when the driver behind me kept a safe distance. I do not like it when cars follow too closely. There was no one behind me. I relaxed all the more. I would be home, soon. I was grateful the office is so close to the house. I enjoyed going home, at lunchtime, when the children were young, and Patricia was there to raise them. It kept spark alive, in our marriage. I know there are couples whose love life waned, once children came into picture. It was quite opposite with us. I found my wife even more desirable, after she began to have kids. We were making love when she went into labor with all of our children.

I made the right turn into our subdivision, drove to the end of the entrance street, and parked the car. Patricia and the girls parked their cars in the garage, while the men parked, elsewhere. It was safer that way. They never had to come out to cold or heat when they wanted to leave. We loved pampering those girls. I stepped out of the truck, retrieved my briefcase, and headed for the back door. I did this when I did not want to be disturbed and my mind was on my wife. Our bedroom was off the spiral staircase of the kitchen. I walked onto the deck and unlocked the patio door. As I stepped inside, I could smell the scent of chocolate wafting down stairs. I walked up the steps, as I loosened my tie and unbuttoned my shirt.

I could feel myself growing hard, inside of my slacks. I unzipped them, to give myself room. I unfastened my belt, as I slipped off my loafers. The smell was much more intense, leading to our master suite. The door was ajar, as I approached it. I leaned my head to the side, to get a peek into the room. I saw my gorgeous wife, sprawled on the California King, with a sheet pulled across her pelvic area.

I noticed the cake, as I stepped inside. It lay across her belly. The chocolate was a striking contrast to mocha tones. I slipped off my shirt, pants and underwear, before reaching the bed. I pulled the undershirt over my head, while I leaned to kiss my wife's waiting mouth.

"*Deliciosa.*" I whispered, into her lips.

"You haven't tasted the cake, Morris."

"I do not refer to cake, *querida*." I kissed her breasts and nibbled her erect nipples.

"Mmmmm, that's nice." She moaned.

"*Si, mi amor*. It is." I traveled further until I reached the cake. It was good. I took my time, ate all of it, and I licked the plate.

Patricia turned around for me to enter her, from behind. She never ceased to amaze me. I do not grow tired of her. On the contrary, I grow more attracted, with each passing day. I held her hips and pulled her gently to me. She rocked her hips to meet thrusts. We were in sync. I felt rhythmic waves on her vagina walls, squeezing and sucking at my member. Her back arched, as I touched the right spot. I kissed her back, just as she reached an orgasm. I released myself, as she slid down on the bed. I rolled to the side, to embrace her in the afterglow. We remained this way close to an hour, just enjoying each other and the feel of our bodies touching. We rose, showered and dressed. I heard someone come into the house. If Keyvaughn knew what is good for him, he will have enjoyed the pleasures of his woman, just as I have done. It is a great release after a hard day.

As we walked down stairs, hand in hand, I noticed Morris, Jr. seated at the kitchen table. It felt good to see him, here. He had been spending his evenings, with his wife, as he should have been. It had been over a year since we have been graced with his presence at the dinner table. I could see something lurking behind his eyes. I was not ready to address it. So, I ignored it, for now. We walked to, and embraced, him.

"Good to have you home, son." I was the first to speak.

"It is good to be back. I was hoping dinner would be ready." He looked at his mother.

"I served your father dessert, first." She smiled at me, as I patted her behind.

She walked to the refrigerator and grabbed a roast she prepared over the weekend. Some potatoes, carrots and string beans sat alongside the meat. She turned on the oven, and then placed the pan inside.

"Dinner will be ready in 45 minutes, baby." She looked in my direction.

"I am famished. I can't wait. Do we have rolls or French bread that can be thrown in a microwave to tide a hungry man over?"

"Anything for you, honey."

"*Gracias.*"

Olivia and Sahara came into the kitchen to greet us. A look of surprise crossed their faces, as they noticed Morris, Jr.

"Hey, Mo!" They chimed, in unison. Those twins seem to always do that.

"Hey, Twin A and Twin B." Mo teased. He called them that since we showed him a sonogram when we found out about them.

"What brings you here, Mo? Where is your wife?" Sahara asked.

I shook my head, in her direction. She got the hint and moved on.

"Mom, did you prepare dinner or should we start dinner?" Olivia asked.

"I have a roast and some vegetables in the oven. It will not be long before we can eat." Patricia said, from the living room.

"I am not that hungry. I still have food from lunch. Don't you still have chocolate cake? I'd love a taste." Sahara reached for the refrigerator handle.

"I am sorry, baby girl. I ate the cake." I advised her.

I heard Patricia chuckle, in the living room.

"Yes, dear. Remember, I told you I was saving it for your father."

"And he ate it, already?"

"Oh yes, sweetie; every last drop. He even licked the plate." It was my turn to laugh.

"The plate was good, too." I added.

I could see dawn appear on the horizon of my children's minds. They turned to each other, and then looked at the two of us. We did not hide things from our children.

From an early age, they understood their mother and I had an active sex life. They were forbidden from walking into our room or sauntering down the hall, without first acknowledging themselves. We had an intercom system installed, so they could call us, then be summoned to the room, if need be.

They smiled at the notion their parents still had sex. I think it gave them a sense of security and stability. They knew that our relationship is solid and one they can count on. We are happy, maintaining a healthy sexual balance, at the same time.

I heard a door close, in the front of the house. Keyvaughn and Cheyenne appeared around the corner. She had the same glow her mother had on her. Keyvaughn had the same sense of peace surrounding him, just as I. We walked into the living room and took our seats around the coffee table. It was time to meditate on our day, before we ate. We sat with our palms upraised and our eyes closed. There was complete silence, as we went into our quiet places of concentration and fully expressed thought.

I sensed agitation, something that had not been there in a while. I realized it was Morris, Jr. It was not uncommon for him to be unable to pull himself into a full-blown meditative state after he experienced a fugue episode. I took his hands, while my eyes stayed closed. I would bring him with me. My breath would regulate his breath. My calm would become his calm.

MORRIS WELLS, JR.

I thought I would be able to sleep better, without the presence of Jacqueline, in my bed. It had been months, since her death, and I still tossed and turned. Perhaps, it had to do with heightened excitement from anticipation of Majestic's arrival. Cheyenne blossomed as he grew within her. She had never looked more beautiful. I continued to chafe under notion I did not have the chance to have a child, with Jacqueline. I detested her for delaying my dreams to assuage her own. It should have been me, beaming with pride, at the swelling womb of my wife. Instead, Keyvaughn and his woman enjoyed the limelight.

I arose from the bed and headed down the hall, to the kitchen. It was predawn hours that I enjoyed the most. This was the time I would wake Jacqueline with an incessant probing of my penis. I wanted entry and she did not fail me. Keyvaughn asked if I utilized skills I learned by studying Tantra. I scoffed. My passion did not want to wait. I should not have to wait to be pleased. If Jacqueline was not satisfied, she knew how to help herself. She wanted to be so damned independent, so I left her to her devices for sexual pleasure, as long as she did not turn to another man.

Keyvaughn would give me a derisive look when I answered his nagging questions about my love life. I did not care. At least, most of the time, I didn't. I wanted to be the lover I imagined my father and brother to be. I could never master the discipline portion of controlling my orgasms. I would get more frustrated, trying. So, I stopped trying. Sahara and Olivia did not have the patience for premature ejaculations, and me. They shunned me and moved on to please each other. There were plenty of others who feared the Wells men, which would oblige me. They knew how to handle the man that I was, so I let them.

As the family business expanded to include call girls, fed from Cheyenne's practice, I used their service, by taking advantage of their sickness. Most of them were sex addicts, seeking assistance. Cheyenne would determine which candidates would take the longest to conform to the ways of society. She would steer them to the business under guise they would work on assignments of self-debasement, as they handled clientele that had been built up. As they drew closer to enlightenment, and self-realization, she would wean them from business and onto a right path of healing.

I sure could use one of those women, right now. I was aroused and I needed release. I contemplated waking one of the twins to ask for a hand job. I nixed that notion, as they would laugh me out of their room. So, I walked over to the cabinet and pulled out a coffee mug. I would distract myself with caffeine and warm drink. The house was quiet, as brew percolated. I imagined my parents making love. I shook my head. My father would kill me, if he knew I thought about my mother, that way.

I was just about to pour coffee, into the mug, when there was a loud banging on the front door. Who the hell would come to the house at this hour of the morning? The banging continued. I, and the rest of the family, raced to see the offending person, prepared to lay into them for disturbing our peace.

"Open up! It's the police." I heard several voices, on the other side of the door.

Before I could get to the knob, there was a thunderous crash and the door splintered. Another push from the other side, and the door gave way. My family rushed to the foyer, as police rushed in and grabbed me.

"Morris Wells, you are under arrest for the murder of Jacqueline Wells. You have the right to remain silent …" The officer read me my rights.

"What is the meaning of this invasion?" My father questioned.

One officer held up a piece of paper, as the other officers placed hands on revolvers.

"We have a warrant for the arrest of Morris Wells, Jr."

"What are the charges?" Keyvaughn asked.

"Murder." The officer replied.

"Keyvaughn…" My father called out.

"I'm on it dad. I have the officers' names, the name of the district attorney who filed the warrant, and the judge who signed it." Keyvaughn had a gift. He had higher than perfect vision and he had a mind to record large amounts of data, in seconds. All he needed was a minute and he could gather names of 20 people, whose names were visible by badge or tag. He and my father practiced, when we were children. His gift is precise and keen.

"You will be hearing from our lawyer." My father stated, as they dragged me out, in handcuffs, to the awaiting paddy wagon.

KENNETH YOUNG

I paced the floor, awaiting word of arrest of the beast that murdered my precious daughter. I have fought long and hard. I called in many favors, in my efforts to get Morris Wells put behind bars. I wanted to hear a jury find him guilty. I wanted them to sentence him to death with immediate exacting of sentence; I wanted to watch him die. He did not deserve to be alive while my daughter is buried six feet under. No father should have to lay his children to rest. My wife was not supposed to endure such hardship, in her life. Morris Wells' family would come to understand what it is like to lose a child. I would do everything in my power to make sure that happens.

Jacqueline's funeral was the most difficult thing our family has faced. Sure, it was not the easiest thing to excommunicate her when she chose to defy my commands to leave that animal. Now, she is dead and we have to live with that truth. She will never have opportunity to come to herself and return to fold, a place she should have never abandoned for the likes of him.

It was hard to explain difference between not seeing her, as long as she remained obstinate in a relationship with the black, and her death. When she walked out the door, that fateful day, I thought her dead to me. I did not grieve or mourn for her absence; she was just out of our lives. We cut off all forms of communication. She was not allowed to call, text, and email or write anyone in this family, when she was in association with the Wells clan. I wiped the dust from my feet. I did everything to persuade her to make the correct choice and reject the asinine notion that she was not like the rest of us. We were on a path of truth. We had God, on our side. All knew this to be truth. In every picture or image of Christ, everyone around him shared our color. The blacks understood that any deity with all power had to be of the most powerful race.

I have read the bible passage, in the book of Revelation, in chapter five, and in verse 15, "His feet were like bronze burning in a furnace." The black people want to believe this is concrete proof Jesus was of their kind. Do they not understand his face was changed when he went to hell? He took on tones of demons. I despised getting into debates about this with other pastors and clergy. Mankind believes what it chooses to believe, as it suits purpose. They want to defame word of God to fit shifting societal views. Do they read, 'Be not conformed to this world, but be transformed by the renewing of your mind'? We ought to hold fast to what the bible teaches; and do not work in confines of being politically correct.

I was a stalwart in my beliefs and I will not be moved. I would not conform, or follow crowds, or get on bandwagons of change. I was not some child that can be tossed to and fro with every wind of doctrine. I have set my face, like flint, against enemies and those in his employment. I would not allow my character and good name be dragged through mud, in unholy alliance with the blacks. This was my reason for severing ties with Jacqueline before word got out that she was involved with trash. My father used to say, 'You lie down with dogs, and you will get up with fleas.' I did not know where the saying derived; I knew I did not want to be linked to running with dogs.

When I thought of my father, a chill ran through me. A wraith of imagery crossed my psyche, memory whittling away at the wall surrounding my past; at least the past that transpired before going to seminary and meeting my wife. I imagined his face, hard and set in a grimace. He was angry. It did not take much to set him off, when I was young. A small mishap or childlike unawareness would send him into rage. He was violent, prone to rancor and cruelty.

I could see it, as if the scene were being played out in front of me. My mother and father are having a heated argument. I cannot distinguish the topic, just that my father is extremely agitated. My mother is attempting to calm him, to soothe his ire, with soft words and touches. He shrugs off her efforts and storms to the fireplace. They are in the den. He picks up the iron used to stoke the fire, and he is flailing it in the air, in front of him. My mother is frightened and she tries to leave the room. But, my father runs after her, blocking her path. He yells expletives, as he rants and raves. His face is dark with anger. He is swinging that iron. Around and closer, he gets near to my mother. She cries, madly. I hear her beg him to put the tool down, sit and speak with her. He refuses. I hear the sound of breaking glass and splintering wood. My mother screams.

A silence falls across the house. I cannot see what is happening, or has happened, in the room. Panic overtakes me and I am still. I am unable to move. I am frozen in place. The door to the den flies open and my father rushes out. He sees me stand in the hallway. He storms toward me and I feel warmness through my clothes as the liquid pools at my feet. I have wet myself. My father's eyes look downward at the evidence of my fear. He grabs me by the collar and slaps me across the face. I can sense danger, in his soul, and I know he wants to harm me. Instead, he throws me down and I fall into urine on the floor. He reaches for the doorknob of the front door, turns it and runs out to the night.

I turn my gaze toward the den. I notice my mother's body lying on the floor. My mind is wild with anxiety. In my mind, I imagine her dead. I remain on the floor, sobbing. I do not know what to do. I hear my mother moan and she attempts to rise from the floor. She groans and falls back onto the rug. She moves, once more. This gives me courage to get up and walk to the den. As I get closer to the door, I see evidence of my father's rage. There is glass strewn across the room. The desk is damaged and little porcelain shards lay on the hearth of the fireplace. I am unprepared to see the condition in which my father has left my mother. She has large welts, on her arms and legs. They are bloody and swollen. A large dark purple bruise forms under her right eye. Her lip is busted.

She whispers, "Go get the first aid kit and the broom, Kenneth."

I run to do what she says and return with the items. She tells me to sit on the sofa, while she busies herself cleaning wounds and evidence of mayhem, which transpired in the room. She approaches the couch and sits beside me with an ice pack in her hand. She places it on my face, where my father struck me. I remember wondering why she did not put it on her face. She notices my wet clothes. Then, quiet sobs wrack her body, as she takes my hand and leads me to my room.

Why were memories flooding back, now? They served no purpose. What could I gain by going back to the dark recesses of my mind, recalling violence of my childhood? Tears stained my face and I wiped them away, angrily. I did not want be bewail a past that had nothing to do with my today.

I sat down and sighed. My father was a good man. He was hit with madness he could not tame. Demons tormented him and carried him away with taunting. I do not know what he dealt with; however, I did know it would get the best of him, from time to time. My mother and I were, both, his outlet. When he yielded to antagonists, he would need to lash out. Near the end of his life, those moments happened more. I could not endure tumultuous waves of his sickness. So, I left for seminary, leaving my mother to live with her decisions. She chose my father. I had no choice of my parents. When old enough to choose, I ran far away.

Seminary was great escape from of my father's demons. I found a stabilizing force within the hallowed walls. Seminary taught me how to break down the bible without having the words alter personalities. One instructor informed us that God wanted to use our character to serve him. Whatever we had going on, he would use in work. The professor told us that change was not needed for those of us in the ministry. We were to use the bible and our mindsets to change parishioners. We were to produce after our kind, no matter how we were. If there was anything that we were dealing with that would prevent us from doing this, it was the dross that should be removed.

Morris Wells was dross that needed to be eradicated from my life. I did not want him to remain alive, as it threw off my balance. I experienced great anguish, knowing he walked around free as a bird. An icy cold permeated my soul and I could not escape its chilly reality. Bitterness took root, deep in the annals of my spirit. It was difficult to read the bible, even more of a challenge to pray for people of my church. I found my prayers being appeals for God's wrath to fall on the Wells family. Jacqueline's death had created a void in our lives. The earth needed to be void of theirs. Their existence was self-serving. They did not offer society anything of worth, as they were a pack of insignificant apes. Morris defiled Jacqueline with his skin; he was color of tar. Pithy. I am reminded of mud, every time I think of him. And the thought of my daughter lying in his droppings sickened me. I wanted to retch, as the images sneaked on me. The images sought to steal any semblance of peace I could gain.

Morris Wells is going to pay for what he has done to this family, a life for a life.

The telephone rang. *The animal has been trapped.*

SARAH YOUNG

I was brought up in a traditional southern home. My mother did not work, outside of the house; she was known as a socialite. She handled my father's business affairs: brunches and tea parties with colleagues' wives, and formal dinners with the men of the office. She kept home spotless; her quiche Lorraine and lemon-peppered duck were perfect. I noticed my father beaming her way at every social gathering, and she was the perfect hostess.

Still, when music faded and the last dish was washed, there was eerie silence that filled the house. Gone was laughter and light banter. It was replaced with fear and foreboding. As my brother and I wanted to keep the darkness away, we would giggle and play, as was children's nature. Yet, my mother would quickly put her finger over her lips, a gesture to keep quiet. My father drank brandy and there was no way to tell when the hell would begin.

It was a never-ending cycle. I remembered praying people would stay a little longer, because that would mean I could see my mother's smile and father's approval. But, it always ended and sadness crept back to the rooms, seeping in corridors like wisps of smoke. The amount of drinking would determine the depth of miasma; from time to time, it was tough to catch one's breath, so thick and murky.

So, as a small child, I determined to marry a man who was the complete antithesis of my father. He would not have brooding mood swings, making it difficult to cross through home. Our children would not be afraid of him, and I would not desire the company of others to avoid bad behavior of a nasty, abusive alcoholic.

Kenneth Young was that man. He swept me off of my feet with his charm and wit. He did not seem to have a dark day, in his life. Nothing seemed to trouble him as his temper was checked. He was a seminary graduate with refined demeanor seeming that of a man of cloth. I felt safe when I was alone with him. He was the perfect gentleman, in private and public. I was ecstatic when he faced my father to ask for my hand in marriage. I felt relief when he dropped down to one knee to propose to me, in the presence of my family. I quickly assented and began to count the days until release from 'southern and proper' hell.

On our wedding night, Kenneth took care with me. He was patient, allowing me to be fully prepared to receive him before he entered me. As a virgin, there was shock and uncomfortable ache when my hymen broke. When I saw blood on the sheets, I was a little taken aback, yet he soothed me by letting me know it was normal and nothing to worry about. He had me lay naked and uncovered on sheets while he gazed at my perfect porcelain skin. Over time, in our marriage, I started feeling uncomfortable under his intent stares.

It wasn't until our daughter, Jacqueline, was born that I realized his obsession with white skin. I would notice his camouflaged glances, as she suckled my breasts. During feed times, he sat, staring unabashedly at her and my bare skin. There were times when I would see him fondle himself while his eyes were on her skin, like he used to do with mine. When I tried to readjust the two of us, to avert his eyes, he would grab my leg, as he sat by my feet, and next he would reach his hand up my skirt to insert a finger in me. He would smile because my body always responded to his touch, even when I didn't want it.

He would spend hours watching Jacqueline sleep. I awoke one night and tiptoed down the hall to see what he could possibly be doing for such a long time. I peered into the room and noticed one of his hands in his pants as he stroked her cheek with his other. I backed away, quickly, confused. Why would he be in our infant daughter's room masturbating? I hurried back to bed, tears coursing down my face. I climbed in bed, burying my head in my pillow to stifle the cries. Later, when he came to bed, he reached for me and I turned toward him. I needed to feel him inside of me. It was like an anecdote to poison I felt sear through my veins. He still wanted me in that way and my body wanted him.

One Saturday afternoon, as he prepared a sermon for the following morning, I went to wake Jacqueline from her nap. I put her on a dressing table and then I undressed her. Her skin was as white as mine, I knew this, but I wanted to see what he saw in our daughter. I turned her over and next I rubbed her bottom. I touched her legs and feet; she cooed. I placed her on her back and looked deeply in her eyes. I wondered if she had cast a spell on her father. I saw nothing except my beautiful angel. I put a fresh diaper on, and took her to the rocker to nurse. I rocked and sang softly, as she suckled. My mind wandered to her father's frequent night visits and something broke, in me. I held my baby girl firmly with one hand and lifted my skirt with the other. I closed my eyes and imagined.

The sound of Kenneth's office door closing startled me. I stopped rocking, pushed my skirt down and removed Jacqueline from my breast. I felt queasy and sick, all of a sudden. I stood up quickly, and felt flush. I sought something to steady myself, just before everything went black.

I awakened to a cool cloth on my forehead and Kenneth fanning me. I sat up, with a start, as I remembered Jacqueline was in my arms prior to fainting.

"Shah, quiet sweetie. The baby is fine. I walked into the nursery just before you went down and I grabbed the two of you. Neither were hurt. I may have wrenched my back, but that is a minute thing. Are you feeling alright?" The look of concern was endearing. All I could do was cry.

As we buried our lovely angel, I thought back to that day. She was now in a coffin, serene and so quiet, just like when she would nurse at my breast.

I did not think of the fact that she had been with Morris Wells, like Kenneth did. He was obsessed about his hatred of Jacqueline choosing a black man over him. I pleaded with her to listen to her father, not that I agreed with him, but I was afraid. I didn't want his feeling of rejection to be a catalyst to turn him into my father. Fear silenced me for years.

Some people would think my actions were selfish. I should have confronted Kenneth the first night, but fear was so intrinsically meshed into my psyche … I did not want to become my mother. Yes, I sacrificed my daughter because I didn't know what else to do to ensure my life would not end up like my parents' life. I wanted more and my silence allowed me more. He always wanted me, no matter how many times he slipped off to Jacqueline's room.

M daughter is dead. I mourned her death. I wanted the murdering bastard to come to justice. What kind of mother would I be, if I didn't? But, there was a small, relieved part of me. A nagging sense of competition was being laid to rest. I sighed. I do not think anyone, at the gravesite, heard, or recognized it for what it was, I could now catch my breath.

PATRICIA WELLS

Morris advised we should go down to the Blackwater Ecological Preserve and check on things. We had harvested what could be gathered and packaged the remainder to prepare for the move. The merchandisers were called in and given product to handle. There was too much attention centered on family with a murder inspection underway.

Every one tightened belts. We spent hours in meditation and thought. Cheyenne was focused, and in tune, with her body and her growing child. Her due date was fast approaching; she needed to be peaceful, and at rest for the labor and delivery. I was impressed by her controlled serenity. She was concerned about her brother, yet she had another life to consider. Majestic needed balance, as he prepared for entry to the world.

The twins work greatest in tandem. Their makeup is unique; each required the other to maintain equilibrium. It was much like their father and I. We flow and ebb off the vibe and energy from one another. Each is complement of the other, just as the girl. I love the way our family maneuvered when crisis arose. We did not fall apart or spiral into confusion. We melded into each other and worked as a well-oiled machine.

So, as family business needed a hiatus, we worked to make it happen, quickly. Since Morris, Jr. was in jail, awaiting the trial, Keyvaughn dismantled the building and he restructured the soil to make it sound for replanting. I directed transplanting foliage from other parts of the preserve to the area where our hot house had been. Morris got permits needed to guarantee work was within county judicial limits. As plants were moved from our facility, it would appear to be above board. I was redefining the area and preparing it for a new project, as far as everyone, the public, was concerned.

Cheyenne's department was put on hold, her clients assigned to other psychologists at the Center. There would be no question, as she prepared to go out on maternity leave. She and Keyvaughn had agreed she would take off work, for a year, to focus on Majestic's needs. Tamu Singletary, the center's Chief Executive Officer, was keen to Cheyenne's decision before the situation ran hot. We were going to miss the income generated from the call girl service.

Morris and I thought the call girl service was clever, ingenious, really. Cheyenne approached us, one day; she wanted to add to family business with her training. She developed a plan to provide a steady stream of income for the family, while not fully compromising her clients' disorders. We reviewed the paperwork and we were satisfied her plan would work, giving her the green light to pursue it.

Keyvaughn was smitten, all the more, with Cheyenne once we brought the idea to the family members. I could see the pride and respect, in his eyes, as he listened to her plan; how lucrative it would be. He hugged and kissed her, after the presentation to us. Fire in his eyes could not be missed. Her father and I were proud, as well. All of our children sought ways to build stronger and more financially stable portfolios for the family. We had taught them well.

Work of shutting down the plant neared completion and then my work would begin. I had my students prepare samples for incorporation, once quartering off an area of the preserve. They awaited a command to transform treated soil to a botanical garden to create funds for the university. Morris, Keyvaughn and their crews worked assiduously to create durable surfaces to support the garden.

I heard my cell phone ring, in the distance. I had placed it in my purse, as was my custom when I came to work. I looked at the caller ID. It was Morris.

"Hello, Morris."

"*Hola, bella.*"

"What can I do for you?"

"*Te necesito.*"

He needed me. Stress was trying to creep in camp and it was necessary to regroup and regain focus. I smiled, grateful to be there for my husband.

"I'm in my office, sweetheart. Come up."

"*Gracias, querida.*" He sighed.

I walked to the bathroom to freshen up for him. I never knew what route his passions would take and I wanted to be prepared for anything. Just as I stepped out, I saw Morris down the hall. I closed the blinds, opened my door, and welcomed him.

We lay across the sofa I had in my office and he rested his head on my bosom. His hands we preparing me, yet I was always ready for him. I moaned, as he nuzzled my breasts with his mouth. I felt him hard and strong, as he readied himself to enter me. I opened to receive him and pull him close.

Afterwards, I noticed his creased brow was smoother and his eyes were more relaxed. He had such a great responsibility as the head of family. He set stringent guidelines and expectations on his shoulders. He had to discipline the side of him that sought to unleash itself against every one that got in his way. He was a fierce, mighty opponent for any one who was deemed worthy to come against him. I know there have been times when he exacted severe punishment on people who threatened the sanctity of all he holds dear.

His darker side did not frighten me, in the least. I was enamored with the whole man. I got aroused at the knowledge he could kill and feel no remorse. His danger was a fantastical turn-on and I used it in our fantasy play. I have asked him to use his guns like he would his hands, when we make love. I shivered when I felt the cold steel against my skin and I knew he used it to protect and keep me safe.

"What is going on in that mind of yours?"

"Why do you ask?"

"I can feel your heart racing and I sense arousal on your skin." He kissed my neck.

"Being close and fantasy of your arsenal makes me wet." I spoke into his ear.

He smiled, as his fingers found evidence of my statement. I gasped, as he slid them inside of me. His cell phone rang. It was a distinctive tone, so I knew it was a call he must take.

"*Lo siento, chica.*" He apologized, as he stroked me. "I have to take this call." He licked his fingers before answering the call.

He winked at me; I got a pang in the pit of my belly. I rose to put on my bra and blouse. I grabbed my skirt, from the back of the chair, and stepped into it. Morris came behind me to zip me up. I leaned into his bare chest.

"*Te quiero.*" He stated, as he pulled arms into his shirt and his legs into his pants. I walked to him and zipped his pants. He kissed me on the lips, before he continued his call and left the office.

I lit a candle, as it would not be best to for my students to smell the fragrance of our love making, in the air. I sat at my desk, and pulled out the design plans for the botanical garden we were going to create. It was a concrete diagram with beautiful, exotic flowers and foliage. We transplanted some and we imported others. It was to be a masterpiece, unrivaled in the area.

MORRIS WELLS, SR.

We had a situation seeking to spiral out of control. Alan Getelman was not doing what Keyvaughn pays him to do. He is to ward off police and publicity that disservice this family. The whole matter, with Morris, Jr. in jail, fell on his shoulders. This should never have happened. He is paid too much money to allow slip-ups of this magnitude.

Now, I get a call and I am told Morris, Jr. has been convicted of murdering his wife, Jacqueline. Someone was going to pay. The prosecution had circumstantial proof, to try the case. My son should not be in prison. Alan should have made his release happen. We have to take care of this, now.

I called Keyvaughn and summoned him to the house. Before doing so, he needed to contact people to get to their posts. A plan of action was needed. There would be no correlation between the court case and the 'accidents' about to go down. I would handle the judge. Keyvaughn would take care of Alan. Since they had chosen to come up against our family, their families would be dealt with.

I had a very difficult time controlling the rage that built up, since the onset of this business of Morris, Jr. and the murder. *Me importa un bledo,* I remember telling Alan, when he stated the authorities had enough evidence to hold and take him to trial. He was to do everything within his power to get my son off. He was to pay off whoever needed to ensure Morris, Jr. got back into the fold. Instead, Alan allowed him to get convicted. My blood was boiling. I wanted to punish everyone involved. I needed to see them suffer and die. I wanted to boil water in a cauldron and cook the judge's children. I wanted someone to brutalize Alan's wife and pillage her goods, while he and his children looked on, and then he would be sawed in half and his body would be dissolved in acid.

The more I thought, the darker and more sinister my imagination became. My body trembled, as my anger grew hotter. This was a situation I would not call Patricia with, as this was not favorable to pleasure.

I felt like I would hurt her and that is the last thing I want to do. I would not be able to live, with myself, if anything happened to her, especially, by my hand.

Keyvaughn walked through the door. I met him in the foyer and we walked into the living room, together. We formulated plans to have people, on our payroll, carry out carnage on Alan's family. Once they were taken care of, the trigger person would bind Alan, hand and foot, and then call Keyvaughn to finish him off. It was our hope that he would be crazed with grief and remorse. His mind would break, while he witnessed his wife's debacle. His soul would splinter at the devastation we wreak on his family. He would beg for mercy into death, but it would not come fast. It would look like an invasion, as men burglarize and vandalize other homes in the area.

In the meantime, across town, I would have a sniper posted in the neighborhood. He would pick off random people, in the area where the judge lives. He would shoot into the homes, plus that of the judge, so shots that kill him and his family appear to have come from the same gunman. I will be waiting for the judge when he arrives home that day. I will have murdered all his family members and put them, throughout the house. He would not know what to do, as he walked up on each of them, one by one. His phone lines would be severed and his cell phone would have been stolen, by one of our people in the courts.

The acid in my stomach churned. I needed an antacid to ease the disruption. I was not accustomed to stress affecting me. I had to reign myself in; I was in warrior mode. I looked to kill as many people as I could. I wanted to strike while the iron was hot. I sensed the panther in Keyvaughn prowling just under the surface. He sought to be unleashed. He wanted to maul and mangle, and savor the meat. I would give permission to do whatever he willed. Leave nothing to recognize, not even the bones.

Once my anger cooled, we would send a clean-up crew to dispose of bodies who touched our wrath, together with innocent bystanders who would fall during the fray. Incidentals are a part of this line of work.

It cannot be helped. There would be some casualties, of war, having nothing to do with battle. They will have no alliance. They will, simply, be in the wrong place at the wrong time.

Sharp shooters and paid assassins would be rewarded for diligence and precision; and then hop on planes back to Bolivia, Peru and other South American countries. We would send for others, once they are safely to their lives and families. They will be upstanding citizens, in their villages and communities. Funds would be established for each of them, in their native land, to live and make merriment in whatever form they chose.

A plan was set in motion. The players were on board and they were ready to execute. Guerillas were dispersed and waited signal to carry move ahead with the plans. Every one had disposable cellular devices to alert them in time. Unmarked guns and hand-made bullets were being used, so there would be no way to trace the evidence.

The last call was made. I was in a stolen car, heading to the judge'. Keyvaughn was heading to Alan. War began. Casualties were reported. We kept count of casualties and where each one was located, so the people in charge of disposing of the dead would know where to go. Traffic was of no concern, as it was just before rush hour; it was dark at this time of season.

I notified clean-up crews to go in to clear everything, except for the judge's family. They needed to be there when he arrived. I wanted him to see the madness he had brought on, before he met the same. He was, indirectly, involved so he would have satisfaction of a swift end to miserable life.

As I waited in the judge's home, I received calls that everything was taken care of and players were on their way to the airport. Most of them would leave on the same flight, with connecting flights in Atlanta. Weapons were disposed. I sat, staring at the bodies of a woman and two teen-aged boys. The judge must have began a family, later in life. His children were younger than I imagined. He and his wife seemed close in age. It was becoming more common to have women of advanced maternal age. I was glad we chose to have our children, in early years of our marriage. I love that they are grown and we can still enjoy each other. We were still young enough to enjoy our grandchildren, play with them and take them on vacations. I did not see the judge and his wife being afforded this luxury.

I heard the key enter into the lock and the chambers clicked to open. The doorknob turned. I felt the hairs on my arms rise. My heartbeat steadied and my pulse calmed. I am made for this; created to be a stealthy killer. The door opened. The judge walked in. He closed the door and placed his keys on a tray, on a foyer table. The lights were turned on, yet I stayed cloaked. I wanted to witness him discover his family's bodies. I saw his hand come to his mouth to stifle the scream that burst to come forth. He trembled, as he raced to the telephone, another body. A high-pitched yell erupted. He backed up and tripped over the last body, that of his wife. I saw him careen out of control. His equilibrium shaken, he began to fall, right into my arms. I relished in the surprise as he realized who I was, just before I placed the gun to his head and pulled the trigger.

PRESTON LAMBERT

I am a man of great conviction, borne of a man with the same paradigm. He instilled in our family the need to address a higher power, as we are but mortals. We are incapable of making our own destinies, in that no matter how we plan, we cannot account for every unknown variable. God is the higher being that we attribute the honor of acknowledging we are created beings that will never own the wherewithal to mastermind our world and the worlds we cannot see. He is the sovereign ruler of all, as the universe is too complicated and intricate to be established at the hands of us humans. With this belief system, I walk worry free, because I am ultimately not in charge of my life. A plan has been put into action, before the foundation of the world, before I was formed in my mother's womb, that I could never dismantle.

It is awesome and mind-blowing that I can do nothing to alter my course, as long as I know I am not the end all that ends all (as my father used to say). This belief system held my family as one, when our patriarch died. Our lives were affected, my mother, sister, brother, grandmother and I. There was no denying we would be a little less, without the guidance of Joseph Lambert. Yet, our faith in God, the unseen spiritual force, gave us strength to endure grief of losing one so dear. A blind trusting, the substance of things hoped for as well as evidence of things not seen, kept us together and built us up, when we thought we could not go on.

His presence is as real and tangible as the wind. We do not search out the source of air current, yet we never deny existence. However, mankind has spent centuries trying to discount God, maintaining that we cannot see Him. He can be felt and experienced. He can move the unmovable and sweep away mayhem in our lives, in the same manner as the tempest. On especially blustery days, the wind can be heard. The same holds true for God. When things seem their bleakest and there is upheaval around, God's presence can be heard. He hovers over mayhem, seeking to bring order in the midst of chaos. Mankind has harnessed power of wind and we use it in many different fashions. It blows leaves, inflates tires, powers the buildings, and extinguishes fire. Wind can create a drag to impede our progress, as well. There are times we forge, full speed ahead, and there is danger in our future. The wind, or pneuma of God, His very presence, slows us; He wants our attention to be more focused on what is happening around us. He wards off danger, by creating drag.

My foundation in God upheld me when I wanted to go my route, choose my path, for life. I wanted to be impatient and not wait on timing of the Lord, when it came to big decisions in life; like finding a wife. I know what you are thinking, *what does God have to do with choice of women?* Well, if I were left to myself, I would have chosen a woman to fit into my life, right now. I would not have taken into account this woman should be able to fit into where I head. As my grandmother, Salester, used to say, *only hindsight is 20-20, Preston.* We tend to forfeit our futures for the brief pleasures of current moments. God knows everything. I choose to believe. It works for me. It has worked for my family and friends who have tried it. He knows what is best for me and who will best fit the bill for my present and future.

My patient wait, on the Lord, rewarded me in a way I never imagined. I have a wife that supersedes my wildest dreams. And I have had some wild dreams. Who hasn't? Her name is Damaris Lambert. She is my good thing; that is what God calls the wife He led me to choose. She is intelligent, sexy, beautiful, and confident. We are in love deeply, on a spiritual level, as well as a physical one. We exude love of God. Our family and friends tell us all the time. My best buddy, Micah Alexander, says he is happy because he sees Damaris makes me happy. And the icing on the cake; he is married to her best friend, Ariel. They are members of the church my family attends, along with their twins, Nassara and Nasir.

Micah and I decided it would be good to give back to the community, so we joined prison ministry at church. We ministered to some and mentored to others who are incarcerated, no matter the reason. We are taught never to judge, because as men, we understand hormones can become out of control and cause us to make irrational decisions we later come to regret. So, it was time to visit inmates at Norfolk City Jail. We were excited, as there's a group of new convicts, since we last visited.

We took Micah's Infiniti and headed from the church. We did not turn on the radio or engage in menial chitchat when we were on route. This was ministry and we needed to focus to hear, clearly, what God desired for the men we would visit. We prayed, in the Spirit, the moment we got in the car. He was driving, so I turned my face toward the passenger side window. I did not want distractions.

I heard the voice of the Lord speak to me last night. He advised there would be a special inmate for me to speak with. He said there would be a connection between us, one that cannot be disclosed right now. He was ready to hear what God gave me to say.

Micah turned on East City Hall Avenue, and pulled into the parking lot. We stepped out of the truck and waited for other men to arrive. We wanted to walk into the jail, together. When the men parked their cars, we put on a united front and headed into the building. I felt the Holy Spirit. He was preparing me for the man that had been prepared for this moment. I wondered if I was going to plant a seed or water a seed planted by another? I heard God say, *you will plant and water this seed, Preston.* I mentally assented to the charge.

We got a list of inmates that agreed to ministry. Each of us had a copy of the list. I perused it, running my finger along the page. *Morris Wells, Jr.* The name jumped off the page. It was almost as if it had been highlighted, for me. I approached the cell group leader and told him God told me Morris Wells was the man I was to speak with. He nodded. He heard the Lord, too. We were in agreement.

The guard led us to an open area much like a conference room, where we held our meetings, bi-weekly. I took a seat at a small table, near the end of the room, while praying in the Spirit. Micah took a seat, along the opposite wall. He was in ministry mode, as well. God has done an awesome work, in his life. He has much to be grateful for, especially during this last year. He had made several mistakes that could have cost him, dearly. He remained in grace and let mercy and forgiveness of God overwhelm and bring him back to a place he was to be. He was a changed man, evident in everything he did. He understood responsibility as head of his household, as husband and father. I was proud. I knew my father would be, as well.

The inmates began to file in. I noticed a good-looking man step inside of the door. He looked around, anxiously. He seemed uncertain and I saw doubt crease his brow. I felt nudging of the Holy Spirit prompt me to approach. I walked his way. He was wary and cautious. He looked frightened and alone. I was careful not to startle him.

"Morris?" I asked, as I extended my hand in greeting.

He took my hand, giving me a firm shake. He was not an average criminal. I felt a judgment rise in me; *he must be guilty of irrational behavior that could have been prevented, if he had taken a moment to think*. I, at once, checked myself. I should not assume or be critical. The man would speak and allow God to help me discern.

"Hello." He put his hands in his pocket.

"My name is Preston Lambert. Let's take a seat at that table, over there." I pointed to the direction from which I had just come.

We walked over to the table and we took seats. Guards positioned everywhere in the room; standing ready, in case something got out of line. I sat, silently. I wanted to give Morris the opportunity to settle down, maybe ask a question. I was right to wait.

"So, what is this all about?" He began.

"What do you mean?"

"I want to know what this men's group is all about. I heard another inmate talking about it and he sounded excited. I want to see what an inmate is excited about while being incarcerated." He sat back and he looked at me.

"Well, we are here to talk about whatever it is that you would like. We are not here to sit in judgment or to force our beliefs onto you. I can only imagine the questions I could have, if I were in here."

"What kind of questions would you ask, Preston?" He looked intently into my eyes.

"First of all, I would ask myself if there was anything I could have done, differently, to prevent me from being in here, in the first place." I looked back.

Morris began to open up. "I asked myself that too. The only conclusion I could come up with was I should not have been born."

"What makes you say that, Morris?"

"If you knew my family, you wouldn't ask." His laugh was dry and unfeeling.

"I do not know your family. So, I am going to rely on you to fill me in, if that is what you want to do." I leaned in, to signal I was interested and fully engaged.

"My family has high expectation; ones that I cannot meet. Since I was a little boy, their goal was to beat the family dynamic into me. I had to think the way that they thought and do things the way they did. We were allowed to choose professions, but it was never a freewill choice. It was controlled. I was influenced my complete life, by a loving father and caring brother." Morris fought tears.

"It's interesting you use the term, *never a freewill choice*. I, too, was brought up in a family with a strong belief system; a set of core values we were expected to live up to, while we resided under their roof. But, God gives us the option of freewill. As an adult, I realized that what I was taught to respect, as a child, I still did. I chose to respect it. There was no fear of reprisal, if I did not."

"Well, good for you. I belong to a family of ruthless narcissists. We are taught to care about nothing if it does not benefit the family dynamic. It is about self-love, and not in a healthy way, mind you. We were encouraged to seek out our every pleasure in our family structure. Our careers were selected to benefit a family crime. We are illegal drug growers and distributors. We also have an illegal prostitution ring. We are also geting into money laundering. My twin sisters are accountants."

"That is a lot to deal with. The pressure must be over the top." I added.

"You cannot imagine. We all have Master's degrees in our fields. I am a Chemical Engineer, my father is a Civil Engineer, my brother is a Geotechnical Engineer, and my mother is an Ethno botanist. I already told you the twins are accountants, and my other sister is a Psychologist. She is, also, pregnant with my brother's first child." He leaned back and looked into my eyes. He searched for shock or surprise. He wanted to see if there was undercover judgment. There was none.

"You are a family of overachievers. What do you do to de-stress?" I asked.

"Well, my father is a master of Tantra and he is also a yoga instructor. As children, we became highly skilled at meditation and relaxation techniques. He is from Bolivia, so we have a never-ending supply of coca leaf we have chewed since we were in high school. It left us euphoric and relaxed. My mother made coca leaf infused tea, for us to drink whenever we felt overwhelmed. I was drinking the tea, often." He laughed.

"Were you able to find yourself within the confines of the Buddhist religion?" I asked.

"I didn't fully embrace it all. I have a side of me that resists the disciplined side of practice. I was never allowed the abandon of teenaged rebellion. I am not saying I would have been a better person, for it. I am saying that it could not have hurt to get it out of my system, rather than to suppress it, at every juncture. It seemed as if we were never given opportunity to desire control, it was dumped on us." He fidgeted in his chair.

"So, how do you think your outcome could have been different, if you had chance to be reckless when a young man?"

"I don't know." He stated matter-of-factly.

"Can I offer something to you?"

"I have nothing to lose, Preston."

"There is a God that designed your life to be one of success, without stress. He took on fault and bore burden of every sin you could commit. He understands the plight of man and knows we need help to do what is right. In and of ourselves, we will never measure to supreme standard. The bodies we possess, by reason of our birth, seek their way and are unruly. So, God chose to give us a Helper, one who takes residence inside of us, and helps us take the reins of our lives back, the life God knows is best for us. We could not think of perfect life, on our own. We can never think of all of the variables. He has taken guess work out of it." I felt God's power overtake me.

"There is a God that cares enough about me to plan my life, and then allow me the freewill to accept it or reject it?"

"Yes, sir." I answered, simply.

"How do I meet him?" Tears formed in his eyes, yet they did not spill over.

"He is in this room. Can you feel air from the air conditioning?" I put my hands up to demonstrate.

"Yes."

"God is much like that. He is everywhere and in everything. You feel Him inside, like skin feels air conditioning. Does that make sense?" I waited for reply.

"Yes."

"What you have to do is say YES, to the gift of salvation; a complete healing and washing of your mind, body and spirit. It is as simple as A-B-C. Admit that you cannot do it on your own, that you make mistakes and fall short. Believe in the gift, that it can clean up any mistakes, past, present and future. Believe God made a plan for you to succeed and live carefree. God died in your place, took punishment you should have gotten, then He got up and returned to heaven to wait your presence. With that knowledge you can confess that Jesus or God did that, making Him Lord of your life, because He knows everything; things we could never know." I looked at Morris.

"You made it sound, so simple. I have a lot of stress and there are other things that reside on inside of me. Is God willing to evict them, so He can take up residence?" His eyes implored me.

"Yes."

"Well then, sign me up!" Morris exclaimed. It was the first sign of peace on his face.

"Take my hand. I will pray with you, much like meditation you spoke of, except we get to talk to God and He wants to speak back to us."

Morris took my hand and I lead him in the sinner's prayer. We talked about what he could expect the first few days, weeks and months. I assured him I would write and visit him twice monthly, for the duration of his stay. I left my phone number with him and let him know he was free to call any time that he required encouragement. I gave Morris an amplified bible and a new international edition. I explained the value of knowing what he was reading. One bible was in laymen's terms and the other one broke down words to help make sense. I advised him God would do the rest, from inside out. No matter his current situation, he was a free man, inside.

We stood and Morris embraced me. I could feel weight lifted from his soul. This man, educated and hardworking, was letting go of years of control. Although there were no tears, I felt a sense of cleansing. He wasn't fully convinced, but he needed more than he had. He would need God's grace and my patience, to see him through.

As I hugged Morris, the guards began to move in, but I waved them away.

CHEYENNE WELLS

There was much going on, in our family. It was taking everything that my father had taught me, to stay on level keel and even playing field. Majestic had filled my uterus to its capacity and my ribs were sore, yet I would not change a thing. I loved being his host. I would never regret this pregnancy; even with aches and pains as my constant companion, these two months.

After the event at my obstetrician's office, I contemplated natural birth, drawn to the drug free aspect. I watched a woman give birth on a seat of a toilet. I was sure I had more stamina and gumption than she. I discussed it with Keyvaughn and mother, and they were willing to support me. My due date was fast approaching; I had one more week. I was excited. Keyvaughn was excited. The family talked of little else for the past couple of weeks. With Morris in jail, we realized there was nothing we could do about it, so we made the best of what could be a bad situation. I was glad we had something good to focus on.

I know Keyvaughn and my father had some dark knight moments, because they tended to be amorous. They spent most waking hours looking to us to help them regroup and stay focused on tasks. There were occasions when both of them came home, looking for my mother and I. We would retire to chambers and give our men what they needed. The haze, in their eyes, would be gone; at least momentarily.

I felt more cramps than normal, these past hours. I attributed it to Keyvaughn's well-endowed member. Do not get me wrong. I loved his piece. I hold it sometimes. It fascinated me. It was beautiful. At times, I wondered if my father had a magnificent package. I am not attracted to my father or anything. I wondered if he passed the penis down to Keyvaughn. I wondered if my mother was as in love with with my father's penis as I am with Keyvaughn's.

I have patients who had relations with their fathers. They talked about how they enjoyed the sex. There are more than a few. Some were driven by sickness to seek brothers, fathers, and uncles for sexual relationships. Some began to compare the family members and upset the ranks.

These, I sought when I wanted to do my part in family business. They had harmful affiliations with penis, in that they did whatever they could to check one and see how it compared with the next one.

I visited the kitchen for a glass of water, to work on getting rid of the cramps. They were beginning to become irritating. I sat down, at the table, to drink the water. I heard my parents' bedroom door open and saw my mother emerge, looking absolutely beautiful. Wells' women were graced with wonderful skin; and it looked even better after special attention from our men. She was so regal. She carried herself like the queen that she was, at least in our world.

"Hello, Mommy."

"Hello, Cheyenne."

"You look lovely." I smile.

"As do you." She smiled, in return.

"Can I get you something?"

"Do not be silly. Is there anything I can do for you?" Concern crossed her brow.

"No ma'am. I am sipping some water, as I am cramping. I think it has to do with sexual frequency with Keyvaughn." I drank from the glass.

"Hmmm. Do you think that is all it is? I see your abdomen hardening, from here." She walked to me and put a hand on my belly.

"Yes. The Braxton Hicks contractions have been doing their thing." I smiled and put my hand on top of hers.

"Have you been timing them, Cheyenne? You could be in labor." Thrill spread across her face.

"You think so?" I shrugged. "This has been going on for a while. They are bearable; more annoying than anything."

"Do you feel pressure in your vaginal area, sweetie?"

"I have. I think it has to do with push outs that happen when I orgasm. Sometimes they can last for hours." I shivered at delicious thought, bringing on a pang and cramping episode.

My mother smiled. She knew what I was talking about, it seems.

I grabbed my belly. This one seemed a bit, odd. It lasted a bit longer and the pressure in my vagina intensified.

"Cheyenne, let's go to your room and let me have a look." My mother took my hand and we walked to the back of the house.

I stepped out of my panties and raised my skirt. I sat on the bed and lied back with my legs open. In that moment, there was more cramping and I had to bear down to help alleviate the uncomfortable feeling. I heard my mother gasp.

"What is it, Mommy?" I reached down to touch myself, hoping she did not see any residue from lovemaking. A gush of water flooded out of me.

"Cheyenne, I see Majestic's head!" She ran to the bathroom to open the linen closet. She reached in my nightstand to get some white thread and scissors. She pulled her cell phone out of her pocket and dialed, 911, as she placed dry towels beneath me.

I did not panic or feel alarmed. I was calm. I placed my hands on my knees as I raised my legs. I was ready to push to meet my baby; I was overwhelmed with love. The child Keyvaughn and I created would grace us, in minutes. I wanted Keyvaughn to be here, but thought of him coming home and to see us waiting for him sounded good.

"My daughter is 39 weeks pregnant, her water broke and the baby is crowning. She is pushing, as we speak." She propped the phone on her shoulder as she placed her hands on my feet. She pushed them back, as she told me to bear down. "Yes, she had obstetrical care for full pregnancy."

I heard the front door open, as I readied to bear down. My mother called for the person to come to the back because I was delivering the baby. To my surprise, it was Keyvaughn and my father. They made the moment perfect. Now, I needed to do the work so my son, our son, could join us. My man came over to me and he kissed me. I returned the kiss, filled with love. Tears in eyes, I got in 'bear down' mode, once more. With that last push, Majestic fell into my mother's arms. She took a clean towel to dry him. I heard him let out a blustery cry and the room erupted in laughter.

My mother tied the umbilical cord with the white thread and she placed Majestic on my bosom. I was overcome with emotion. I sobbed, as I held my son the first time. I waited so long and time had finally come. He was born in the place where he was conceived. Peaceful and loving members of his family surrounded him. This could not have been better. Keyvaughn slid on the bed, and he wrapped his arms around the baby and me. We cried, as a family.

I heard sirens, in the distance. Soon, there was a knock on the door and someone rang the bell. My father head down the hallway to the front door to escort the paramedics to the room. My mother pulled my skirt down, making me as presentable as possible, under conditions. I beamed pride and love, as they lifted me to the gurney and wheeled me to an ambulance.

MORRIS WELLS, JR.

It had been a few months since I decided to give God a try; I received many letters from Preston Lambert. He had been true to his word, with constant support. With my close-knit family, I had not experienced a commitment to my welfare and well being as I got from Preston. I was grateful to God. There were times when I could not believe I was where I was, in this. I finally found a place where I could rest and not feel like I had to do all the work. Preston said the Lord is ever present to assist me when I feel weak or confused. He did not understand how important that was to hear. My family expected me to be a stalwart. I had to be in control, always. I was never to show weakness to anyone, as it could be downfall to all we had worked so hard to attain.

I pulled out a letter and noticed a prayer attached to it. I skipped to read it first. Preston prayed so well.

Lord, I bless and magnify Your name as God! I thank You for health and strength, as only You give. I magnify Your name, above all in life. You are always BIGGER. There is nothing, in my life or my brother's life, of which you are not aware. There is no situation to take us out of Your sight.

Thank You for being EVER PRESENT HELP as You hide us, safe in arms under Your wing. Lord, when darkness overshadows, You are Light and Salvation. We have no reason to fear because You are with us. When losing direction, Your rod and staff comfort us.

We never have to be anxious, because You know our end from the beginning. You take care of all. You are inherently good; all that comes our way is for our good. We will not presume to know what is best for us, without consulting You. We are Your handiwork. We are vine and You are the Husbandman. You know what to pluck, prune, and pull up. We blossom under Your care, never concerned as You lead us beside still waters, and prepare a table before us, in the presence of our enemies. We are EVER SAFE! We gain confidence knowing You have done ALL the work. You commissioned us to follow You.

Thank You for dwelling amongst us, and devising a plan for that to happen. Thank You for watching over us, as we slumber. Thank You for Your angels to minister to us, Your heirs of salvation. Thank You for every trial and test You groomed us to pass with flying colors. You did not create us to fail.

As we walk through the fire, You work and refine us so to show Your reflection. Thank You for making the call to our loved ones, giving them opportunity to accept the free gift of salvation. Thank You for calling our name and engrafting us into the vine.

I bless Your name, God, for my brother. I thank You for his life and ministry. I thank You for the gift You have placed in him, making him an invaluable member of the Body. I need him, Father.

Thank You for placing him in my sphere of relationships. Thank You for touching his life, making Your presence an astounding force, in his life.

Even as Morris reads this prayer, let Your power rise up, within him. Thank You for loving, blessing, and for favoring him with grace and mercy. Thank You for caring about things he dare not utter, and for allowing Your will be done. Whatever he struggles with, give him peace in knowing You have already worked it out. He is not judged, but loved. Gently nudge him when weary, so he will never become stagnate, slip or fall. The enemy has to lose his hold on him and any part of his life that he is trying to infiltrate. He will NOT succeed.

The blood of Jesus covers him and his family. He is under Your safety arc, as all of Your beloved sheep are. Manifest Your blessings in and through his life, even now, Lord God. Touch his mind, body and soul.

Help him to keep Your commandments and be a beacon to those around him. Give him the words to speak when he is called upon, in the name of Jesus. Hallelujah -- Amen!"

Tears filled my eyes, as I read. I was grateful for this man, my mentor that God placed in my life. He encouraged me when I thought I would not make it. The peace that eluded me, my entire life, was mine. With help God provided, I was able to keep my temper, in check...at least, most of the time. I still wrestled with demons, those that taunted me for so long. Preston told me I would have to resist rising feelings, and call on God to give me strength.

My family knew nothing of my newfound religion. They would laugh me out of the family. I would be ridiculed and scorned for being weak. I did not feel weak. Instead, I felt empowered. I knew a time would come when I must face them, head on, and deal with whatever they threw my way. I hoped I would be strong and courageous. All of my family is strong willed. They ascribe to the law that father put down, but I do not stand in judgment of my family. Where I had been trying to do this all on my own, I realized I have a Helper who makes this easier than I imagined it to be. Not easy, as in a piece of cake, but easy in that work is not all on my shoulders. I just had to submit to the plan and think nothing else, about it. Everything that happens benefits me. Preston helped me to see that.

I finished the rest of the letter. It is good to read that Damaris was doing well and wanted to meet me, if possible. She heard about me and prayed for me, every day. I smiled at notion there was someone that was concerned about my success that does not know who I am.

I would be honored to meet the woman who supported a man who took me under his wing. He was like the big brother I wish Keyvaughn were. He was determined that I be focused and on track, without being demanding and overbearing. I could not imagine Preston beating me over the head, to make me do what he thinks I should do. He wants what God wants for me. There were no hidden agendas, with Preston and other men of the prison ministry. If I were released, I would want to be a member of his church.

When talk of church membership came up, initially, I was a bit wary. I had never been in a church, nor had any churchgoers ever influenced me. My parents made sure we were not broached with the topic, in any shape, form or fashion. Their way was the only way, in our household. It worked for them, so it was what they taught us. I am grateful for love I have for my family and I can receive their love without questions plaguing me. I often wondered if I would be able to measure up to the standard and bar Keyvaughn set for us all. With God, there are no comparisons. We are received and loved with knowledge of who we are and what we are capable of doing. We are unique. We are fearfully and wonderfully made. I do not have to measure up to what man or my family thinks I should do. I am to please God by resting in the fact He planned good things, even in the midst of bad. He knows our outcome and we are safe under His power and knowledge.

Nothing catches Him, by surprise, Preston told me. He is never disappointed because He is fully acquainted with His creation. Wherever we are, God has a direct plan for that place. We are never out of reach, no matter where we choose to go.

I could not get enough of reading Psalm 139. It was as if the psalmist understood and knew me, personally:

You searched me, LORD, and you know me. You know when I sit and when I rise; you perceive my thoughts from afar. You discern my going out and lying down; you are familiar with all my ways. Before a word is on my tongue you, LORD, know it completely. You hem me in, behind and before, and you lay hand upon me. Such knowledge is too wonderful for me, too lofty for me to attain. Where can I go from your Spirit? Where can I flee from your presence? If I go up to the heavens, you are there; if I make my bed in the depths, you are there. If I rise on the wings of the dawn, if I settle on the far side of the sea, even there your hand will guide me; your right hand will hold me fast. If I say, "Surely the darkness will hide me, and the light become night around me," even the darkness will not be dark to you; the night will shine like the day, for darkness is as light to you.

For you created my inmost being, you knit me in my mother's womb. I praise you as I am fearfully and wonderfully made; your works are wonderful, I know that full well. My frame was not hidden from you when I was made in the secret place, when I was woven together in the depths of the earth. Your eyes saw my unformed body; all the days ordained for me were written in your book before one of them came to be. How precious to me are your thoughts, God! How vast is the sum of them! Were I to count them, they would outnumber the grains of sand— when I awake, I am still with you.

If only you, God, would slay the wicked! Away from me, you who are bloodthirsty! They speak of you with evil intent; your adversaries misuse your name. Do I not hate those who hate you, LORD, and abhor those who are in rebellion against you? I have nothing but hatred for them; I count them my enemies. Search me, God, and know my heart; test me and know my anxious thoughts. See if there is offensive way in me; lead me in the way everlasting.

KEYVAUGHN WELLS

The birth of my son changed my life and dynamics with Cheyenne. I came to know love has many levels. There are rooms on each landing, and closets within spaces. My capacity to love increased and swelled far more than thought capable. The word joy does not bear enough weight, when it comes to describing an ineffable sense. My enlightenment and expression of self had broadened. I was open field. My son and his mother ran free within the glade. We are a family.

I wished I were capable of remaining in this state of joy; but there was business of Mo being in jail. The new lawyer set up an appeal, taking longer than I felt necessary. However, I could not rush the process. He assured me there was a loophole to allow my brother to be released. I was promised results and I wanted nothing less than guarantee. In the interim, I visited Mo on often. I noticed he seemed more peaceful behind bars than I ever saw him when he was on the outside. There was an aura of happiness around him, which did my heart glad. I wanted my brother relaxed and in control of himself.

Kenneth Young was fast approaching one of the most deplorable people I had ever encountered. He asked me to quiet him, forever. My father said I could not, nor should I contemplate killing him, at least until Mo was home, where he belonged. His disappearance would be suspect and we could not afford attention. We were already in a position to delay our business, indefinitely. We transferred our product to Bolivia where our merchants sold it. The residual income flowed, but once that was gone; we were left to live off legal means.

Since Mo was in jail, we made his room a nursery. We moved Mo's things to private storage and replaced them with Majestic's layette. He was a good baby and Cheyenne was a wonderful mother. He nursed well and gained weight. His pediatrician said he was in the 16th percentile with height and weight. He was going to be a big boy. He was happy, healthy, loved, and source of much joy. My mother was doting and my father became accustomed to the role of *abuelo* to my little man.

My father and I sat, content, watching the news of random acts of violence that had broken out across the area. There was no evidence to link crimes to each another or families. Police were baffled and on high alert. They set patrols in the area to scan neighborhoods, hoping to bring peace. I hate police and their patronizing air. They did not know they had nothing to do with silence in the streets. But I would not burst bubbles, not yet. I was content with them believing their presence made a difference.

As I waited for Cheyenne to return from feeding our son, I looked out the bedroom window. I noticed a neighbor sitting on the porch of a house across the street. She swung, slowly, as if trying to not disturb the air. She picked up a wine glass and took a small sip. I watched liquid flow into her mouth and saw her put her head back, closing her eyes. It was one of the most sensual things. I sat up and looked directly at her. Her legs rested comfortably over the edge of a swing. Her toes, painted red, looked perfect. I felt myself grow erect while perusing her body.

I rose from the bed and walked over to the window, with just my boxer shorts on, and pulled the curtains back, slightly. I stood, feeling a breeze sweep across my aroused body. Then, our eyes locked. The rocking stopped. With a glass still in her hand, she licked her lips and crossed her legs. She taunted me. She did not know who I am. Does she not know I do not take kindly to being teased? I have never let a woman flirt, and not give her what she asked for. My manhood demanded attention.

"Hi, what are you looking at?" Cheyenne asked as she walked back into the room. Her gaze followed mine. "Really, now?"

I turned to face her; she saw my erection, and said, "Really."

"What are you going to do to help me with this?" I took her hand, placing it on me.

She smiled and spoke, softly. "Why should I deal with something I did not start?" She stroked me.

"It doesn't matter what cause, does it?" I leaned and kissed her passionately.

She moaned and continued to caress me. "Is he going to treat me the same, if he isn't looking for me?" Cheyenne whispered.

I pulled her to me, and grabbed her hair, enough to get a gasp. "Never doubt him."

She placed one foot on the bed, and she led me inside of her. I saw her gaze settle on the woman who had not lowered her eyes. With her hands on my buttocks she began to pull me deeper into her. I kissed her neck and lifted her up, as she wrapped her legs around my waist. I loved the show we put on for our neighbor. I felt her stare on my back, as I slipped in and out of Cheyenne's wetness. The only time the mother of my child's eyes left the woman was when she climaxed. As she clenched me with her vaginal walls, it was as if she begged me to join her, so I did.

We fell back on the bed, no longer caring with woman on the swing. It was just the two of us, as it had been countless times before. My focus was redirected to where it belonged, in her arms and being satisfied by her. I heard that once a child has opened a woman's matrix, the elasticity is never the same. I was grateful it was not the case with Cheyenne. She was still just as tight as a virgin.

"How was your visit with Mo, Keyvaughn?" She nestled in the crook of my arm.

"It went well. I wish there were some news I could tell him about the appeal, but he is in good spirits. He is not troubled, at all." I brushed her hair, lightly.

"Hmmm, that is unlike him."

"It is becoming him, the longer he remains behind bars. I wonder if this was a catalyst for him to learn to center himself."

"That would be great. I know how you and Papi worry about him. He wrestles within himself so much."

"Yeah. I thought he would crack from being away. Instead, he is a quieted soul."

"You let him know the family has punished all involved with his arrest and verdict?"

"What are you talking about?"

"I am not blind or ignorant to tactics the family resorts to when some don't fulfill a promise or come through as expected." Cheyenne smiled.

"Is that right?"

"I know we had something to do with the 'random acts of violence' that happened soon after his trial. I expect nothing less." She looked at me. "I love that you will do whatever it takes to protect the sanctity of family. Morris might not be comfortable with this, but I am at peace with it."

She climbed on top of me and straddled my hips. She rocked back and forth until she got the response she wanted. I put my hands on her thighs, lifted her onto my shaft, and she smiled as I filled her, again.

PRESTON LAMBERT

I sent Morris snippets from sermons, small newsletter articles and blog posts, from time to time. I had a true love for this man whom God placed within my care. I was grateful for opportunity to be on the prison ministry team. It enhanced my spirit in a way I never imagined. I grew closer to the team, including Micah. I aw him blossom and flourish. He was a better man for the mentorship he has undertaken with the inmate God placed with him. He kept up with him and wrote letters. I saw pride, on Ariel's face, when she talked about work her husband did for God.

I can say the same about Damaris. She is such a blessing, to me. She took interest in Morris, almost as much as I had. She baked him cookies and sent him greeting cards. I know she prayed for him and that did my heart good.

Morris,

I imagine the trials and temptations face behind bars. It is tough enough being a man, on the outside. I would love to have more time to sit down to talk with you, face to face. My heart is full; I get a sense you are feeling out of sorts. You have a strong tie to family and teachings. It will be easy for you to resort to old ways of handling things. Please do not deal with emotions, on your own. Talk with God.

I hope you remember you are not alone … your struggle is not yours to bear, alone. God stationed help, inside you. It is help to sustain you through toughest times. Just speak, to Him, from your heart. Don't try to make it sound like what you imagine it to be. He listens to every word. He wants you to share thoughts and tell Him of the difficulties you face.

Do not hang up on guilt or condemnation about your past. Once you decided to give Him a try, He tossed your past into a sea of forgetfulness. He will never remember tour past or bring it up. He presses your mistakes down and buries them in deepest recesses of an ocean called grace. You are free from the strangle hold of things that once were. Walk in forgiveness and don't give your past thought; God does not.

A copy of my pastor's blog is included. Let it sink in and become your new truth. If you have questions or comments, please write them down so you will not forget them when I come for my next visit (which shouldn't be too long). Until then, remain free in mind; that is where it counts most.

MORRIS WELLS, JR.

I read a lot, since Preston sent me content and letters. I knew he was concerned I would sink back, if I were not careful. I expected to get out sooner than later, and I would go back to my parent's house. I wish I had wisdom to keep the apartment I had with Jacqueline. It would be easier to deal with family, if I had my own retreat, to rest my head and mind. I would have no chance to rest, once freed; there would be harassment and jibes about going against our dynamic in search of some ethereal being that very well may not exist.

Instead of worrying about being released from prison, I read a book from the jail's library. It was called 'Blood Dipped'. I read a few pages:

In the beginning, God created, taking time to prepare the earth and heavens prior to man. He communed with man, the part of creation made in His image and likeness. He wanted relationship, with man and woman. The bible states, God and Adam spent time in the cool of the evening. It was during this shared communion God found man and woman hiding in shame of disobedience. God called to them, "Where are you?" It was not a question to which God had no answer; He wanted man to know the state of separation.

We do the same thing, today. We are wired with a sense of right and wrong. We are given freewill to make choices for good or evil. Selfishness leads us to search out and take what doesn't belong to us. Once we conceive idea of forcibly taking on the rights, properties and freedoms of a fellow man, guilt keeps us company. Once we allow what has been done to us, to define us, shame is our comrade. As we make a habit of forced entry and mislaid onus, we are toxic and tarnished, no longer shining with brilliance. An albatross attaches to our ankles, pulling us under into a pit of despondent, sociopathic behaviors.

God has not stopped asking the question, "Where are you?" He has been, since the initial fall, calling out to us to examine where we have traveled within. Do not focus on material things. God wants you to recognize triggers and points of inception where you take an alternate route that has *not been ordained, for your life; the route of guilt and shame.*

Adam and Eve followed an alternate route, with selfish desire. They sought something that did not belong to them. They spent time dwelling on it, stepping off path and onto another's path. Once there, it was easy to assume right to abscond the fruit of a tree that was not theirs. The light of freedom dimmed, and they realized their nakedness, seeking to hide from God.

I imagine God saddened by human choice to focus on what did not belong to them. He had laden them with a continent. He gave dominion of everything, to them. He bestowed His likeness upon man, for him to manage what was given to him. Yet, they turned backs on ownership. They forfeited the gift.

Recall our past, the susceptible moments. Where did we veer off track, in search of something that did not belong to us? When did we embrace false teaching of negative words, allowing them to mask truth, with pockets of insecurity? We do not have to be afraid of what we find. God makes ways out of every wilderness. He opens doors, fashioned for our escape.

Psalm 23 , "Yea, though I walk through the valley of the shadow of death, I will fear no evil, because You are with me." The bible says that darkness is light before God. Even when we feel like we have fallen into pitch-blackness, God is there, lighting our way. He is our Shepherd. He is a lamp at our feet and lights our paths. We should take time for our spiritual vision to adjust to the atmosphere and we will see as God sees. His rod and His staff will comfort us.

God covered Adam and Eve's nakedness with animal hide. They needed covering for their condition. They were no longer able to enjoy freedom, which comes walking in 'what was theirs'. A sacrifice had to be made, in order to provide them with what they needed to hide shame. Blood had to be spilled, for sacrifice. Something died to allow for covering.

When choice is made to latch onto other people's things, something dies, to provide for nakedness. Once death occurs, we are laden with remains, our outer garment. We are identified by what clothes us. When others see us, they describe us by what we wear. And if we have dressed in dead remains of sacrifice, we are unrecognized. We attract things and people, which are accustomed to feeding off dead things.

In God's redemptive plan of bringing us back into fellowship, He decided to become sacrifice. He desires the simplicity of the original plan, over complex concepts we adopt. When we rape and pillage another man's village, home, or person, we give way to thoughts that accompany negative acts, we take on a part of death. God longs for us to take on image and likeness in which we were created. By unselfish forfeit of Jesus and purity of His blood, we are covered with life and all needed to sustain it. The bible says Jesus is the Way, Truth and Life – and His life is light of men.

There is an old hymn, "There is a fountain filled with blood, drawn from Emmanuel's vein; and sinners plunge beneath that flow, lose all their guilt and shame." The blood of Jesus Christ, cleanses us from pall of poor decisions and our embrace of the negativity sown into our lives.

We are washed and cleansed by sacrifice. We are clothed in it. We are stripped of dead remains. "He, Who knew no sin took on our sin and bore them upon the tree (cross)." We are free of the weight of self-seeking. We are free from weight we took on when offended. Why, you might ask? This is what God wants. He does not want us to be heavy laden with guilt and shame, so He made a choice to rescue and wrestle us from of things that bind us.

Accept the sacrifice God made on your behalf. Do not hold on to anything that reeks of death. Choose life, abundant life. Release those things that you have done, no matter how dreadful. Do not be defined by deeds that have been done to you. Ask God to help you free yourself from the cinderblock designed to keep you down, in dumps of despair. No longer accept and welcome guilt and shame as companions. Accept that you are free from Thank God, God...in Jesus' name, Amen.

Before long, it was time for dinner; I had to put the book down. I folded the page over. I was feeling stronger, now, still a bit insecure about what it was going to be like when I got home, but I was certain that I would be able to face it, with God on my side, along with Preston Lambert and other men on the prison ministry team. I was so grateful for them and for time they took, out of their schedules, to come to talk with us. Many inmates said they would not have made it, had it not been for the ministers.

I, for one, would not be where I was had it not been for prayers, encouraging words and visits from the team. I wanted to get a thank-you card to them, once released. I would, also, give testimony at church, and maybe become a member of the prison ministry, if they allowed me.

KENNETH YOUNG

My days filled with murderous thoughts, since the day we put Jacqueline into the ground. I left mind to folly and musings have been villainous. I filled with contempt every time I thought Morris Wells was alive and my daughter was dead. I wanted to hurt someone. I had not preached, since her death. I had not made love to my wife. All I was able to do was devise plans of pain and torture to inflict on those niggers.

It didn't matter they were educated. How much can a baboon descendant retain? They might have been able to fool with the business community, but I was not fooled. I knew their kind. I was taught, by father, what they are and are to be used for by those of higher rank. I had not been able to rest, since I tasted of the ruin between black whores' legs. I brutalized my share of their women, since that bloody bastard killed my Jacqueline.

I was not proud, but my soul was ferocious for revenge and I was unable to get close to the Wells women to pillage them, so I did what I had to with others. I was careful to leave the dirty tramps with enough fear to keep quiet, pummeling their faces and bodies within inches of life. Knowing they were lucky to be alive, they were silent.

I could not get at ease. Sarah had gone to bed. My mind raced and imaginings took over. I needed a release. I could not rest. I was full of wrath and bitterness. I felt like an agitated spirit that needed to roam and fulfill lustful terrorism. I wanted the whole race obliterated or trampled to submission. They did not deserve happiness, while my precious doll lie beneath dirt. I grabbed a jacket and headed past the staircase. The bedroom door opened, slowly, but I did not acknowledge it. I rushed into the night air.

I was like a wild field beast, nocturnal and menacing. I could feel fire rage behind my eyes and the only thing to quench it was to sate its' taste. I drove without clear path. I would know when to stop to unleash my anger. Just in that moment, I saw her. She wore a mini-skirt with fishnet stockings. Her legs were long in stiletto heels that accentuated them. I felt slightly aroused at thought of what I would do to her; how I would hurt her and emblazon the memory of this night forever in her mind. I slowed and rolled down the window.

"How much?" I asked, as I looked around to see if there were witnesses. It was my good fortune this tramp walked the night alone. There was no one in sight.

"Watch you lookin for, daddy?" She leaned toward the driver's side window.

"The works."

"Well, that will be 200 dollars." She held out her hand for the money.

I slapped her hand away. "Not so fast. I didn't agree to your asking price." Bile rose up my throat; the demon would not let go.

"Listen, daddy, do you want it all or what?" She had nerve to sound impatient.

"I want it."

This time when she held out her hand, I reached for my wallet and counted out the money. She placed it in her bosom and walked around to the passenger side of the car to get in. Blood coursed through my veins, as my heartbeat rate increased.

I drove. She put her hand on my crotch, massaging me to erection. She unzipped my pants to free my part from its cramped space. The car swerved.

"Whoa! Take it easy." She whispered, as she leaned her head toward mine. She brushed her tongue against my earlobe. "Drive to the motel around this corner." She pointed her finger to my left.

"I prefer someplace less conspicuous." My voice was husky. Right now, I hated my body for betraying me.

"This is like Burger King, daddy. Have it your way."

I pulled around a corner and parked the care in an alley.

"I don't want any distractions." I turned the ignition off and motioned her to get out of the car. She did, without question.

"There isn't much to be done, back here, daddy. But suit yourself, it's your dime." She took my enlarged penis into her hand. She knelt down and I grabbed her head to shove myself into her waiting mouth.

I felt her throat open to me. She tried to pull back, but I would not allow it. I kept pumping and pumping until I heard her gag. A sinister smile crossed my lips as I thought, *"Yes, choke and die."*

She put her hands on my legs, to push her head away from my erect anger.

"What the f..." She began, but I surprised her with a fist to her jaw.

"Finish the job!" I demanded as I grabbed her head, once more.

She tried to resist. I kicked her in the stomach. She moaned as she fell to the ground. I reached down to pick her up and slam her face into the hood of my car. The whore wanted to scream, but I held her mouth, with one hand, as I pulled up her skirt with the other. I got a wicked thrill as I saw her tears fall down her cheeks and onto my car. She didn't have on panties, so it was easy to enter her. I did so, with as much force as I could muster.

She scratched at the car and squirmed as I tormented her. I slammed her head on the hood, with each thrust. I tore at her flesh with my fingernails, wrapping my hands around her throat. I used her for leverage as I unleashed my anger and frustration. I felt her blood, warm against my penis, as I ripped her from front to back.

"Remember this, black whore." I grunted, as I poured venom deep inside. When I pulled out, she fell limp to the ground. I smiled, as she lay there, lifeless and still. I ripped her skirt off and used the cloth to clean up her blood that was now running down my leg. I spit on her and threw her clothes down beside her.

I looked around to ensure there were no onlookers. I opened the car door and sat on the seat. I took a deep cleansing breath and sighed. The demon was sated, now.

As I backed the car out of the alley and turned onto the street, heading home, the thoughts came rushing. I was not going to find peace, tonight.

I got home, went to the sink in the laundry area, turned on the water, and removed my clothes. I grabbed a washcloth. I freed myself of the terrible stench left from the whore's blood and cheap perfume.

Morning came quickly. I awakened, in my chair, stiff and sore. I could not decide if it was from sleeping in an awkward position or if the aches were from my late night trips. Whatever, I wondered why I could not feel, what should have been, a heavy weight of guilt for what I had done.

I reached into the desk drawer and pulled out a file I kept since Jacqueline's murder investigation started. I did not trust the trial to render punishment I felt necessary, so I pressed police officers and the district attorney's office. I used my clout, as an upstanding man of cloth, and I also spoke with the judge to ensure Morris' conviction. It worked. They threw the book at him, by sentencing him to life in prison. He would never see outside of those walls.

I could not believe my good fortune when everyone involved, oddly, went missing or were found dead after being caught in the midst of some gang war or something. I was glad they were not around, in case they were overcome with guilty conscious, and found a way to blow the deal.

"Kenneth?" Sarah called.

"Yes." I answered, a bit gruffly.

"I don't mean to disturb you, but breakfast is ready."

"I will be down, after I wash up." I pushed back from my desk and thoughts.

MORRIS WELLS, JR.

I had been having a bit of a problem with a certain inmate. The men were always looking to test each other, so I was not surprised I became a target. I tried to walk away, but he did not make it easy. I could feel my training long to unleash, but I knew that was not the way God wanted me to handle things. It wouldn't take long to silence the agitator. Instead, I heard something within myself, a passage that I read, with Preston.

"Bless those who persecute you, who are cruel in attitude toward you; bless and do not curse them. Rejoice with those who rejoice, sharing others' joy, and weep with those who weep, sharing others' grief. Live in harmony with one another; do not be proud, snooty, high-minded, exclusive, but readily adjust to people and things, and give yourselves to humble tasks. Never overestimate yourself or be wise in your own conceits."

That passage was in the book of Romans, the 12th chapter, in the 14th, 15th and 16th verses. Preston impressed upon me importance to memorize the scriptures, we discussed. He said repeat them. I stumped on a word, here and there, but overall, I could recite scriptures and also understand meaning. Preston called it meditating. He related it to rumination; the way a cow chews, swallows, and then regurgitates cud to chew it, again. I was glad I listened to his advice; it came in handy, today.

I loved the way God ordered His word to publish to us. I loved His forethought, along with His direction and plan for the lives of people accepting the sacrifice of His Son. I loved His order and desire for peaceable living. He is concerned about us and wants us to place care in the lives of others. If this were not so, He would have not said it. He let the Romans passage be highlight of what He wanted to be known. He knew there would be some persecution, persecutors and persecuted. His desire is for all to be saved from ties that bind us to a wrong way of thinking or doing things. The persecutors need prayer.

One day, Preston asked me a question, which rang in my mind, *"Are you praying?"* I did not pray at the time. I wanted my persecutors to be exterminated, as that is my family's way of handling things. I had to remember Jesus on the cross. His words about were: "Father, forgive them for they know not what they do." I have to remind myself that my prayer is not excusing the persecutor. It is acknowledging they are unclear on the 'soul' ramifications of their actions. This is what I needed to keep in mind when I persecuted or witness to others persecution. The soul ramification is not always clearly indicated to those who are persecuting others.

I would pray for them just like Jesus did for those who sought to kill Him, and not curse them or wish them harm. They needed the grace of God applied to their lives, just like I did. To inspire me, I was blessed with more information from Preston:

"Do you know what it feels like to have on clothing that is too small, for you? Maybe you have a pair of shoes you've outgrown? This is how it feels, to our spirits, when we live with thoughts of what has been done to us, who owes us apology, who should repay us for wrongs against us. We are

constricted, bound to an event, rather than to God, Who can free us from our pasts. He tells us to forget things that are behind, and press toward our future. He says, we are to take things day by day, knowing He has made provision. When Jesus spoke to people, about being free, they perceived a natural bondage, thinking to generations of slavery and exile. They bound to tradition. They bound to religion. They bound to rules and their way of things. But, Christ wanted them free from guilt of trying to be "perfect" through laws and restrictions. He wanted them to experience the freedom in knowing God loved them, enough to pay penalty and rescue them from law of sin and death. He wanted them to grasp He sought a rapport. He wanted them to draw near Him, through the gift of His Son. He wanted them to draw near the mountain to worship and hear from Him. (Exodus 19: 10, 11 "And the LORD said to Moses, "Go to the people and consecrate them today and tomorrow. Have them wash their clothes and be ready by the third day, because on that day the LORD will come down on Mount Sinai in the sight of all the people." {New International Version}) As

He addressed the crowd, they refused to let go of status quo. We tend to follow the same paths. Do you often resort to old ways when trouble arises? Do you go back, when you are pressed up against the wall? Maybe it's fear keeping you from accepting change. God is looking to come, directly, into our circumstances. He wants us free from fear, to come to Him, and hear Him. Christ came so we would not need a veil between God and us. He is the Way, Truth, and Life.

MORRIS WELLS, SR.

I have gone over my son's trial, since I heard the verdict. Something was strange about how it went down. There was too much evidence. Morris, Jr. knew to do a better job than what they presented to the jury. The judge seemed eager to sentence my son to life behind bars. Alan Getelman could have done more, but prosecution and arresting officers worked in tandem, with precision. It's not often that a murder trial is so cut and dry.

I never asked my son if he killed his wife. I don't care whether he did it or not. What I did care about is he was paying for it, based on word of someone, else. We do not bend to society's whims. We make our rules, and follow our commands. And when someone wanted otherwise, we dealt with him or her. It is not for others to set fate for the Wells' family. We are gods of our own destinies.

I put new people on the case. I called my Bolivian contacts.

My son's life was at stake.

I needed my wife. She was the person who could bring me peace, when I had so much on my mind. There was nothing that could be done, now. I could not have my mind cluttered with regrets or anxiety. I needed a clear head to execute. Morris would not have many more nights away from family.

I walked to the kitchen and began to climb the stairs to our bedroom. I could hear the shower running, as I drew closer to the entryway. I removed my clothing and placed it in the hamper. I sauntered to the bathroom, leaned in the doorway, and watched water cascade down Patricia.

She must have felt my gaze, because she turned to me and smiled. After all these years, it still took my breath away. She opened the shower door and invited me in. I stepped in. The water ran down my back. Its warmth felt good and soothing to tense muscles. Patricia took my face into her hands and pulled me in for a long kiss. I wrapped her in my arms.

"You feel good, baby." Patricia breathed, in my ear.

"As do you, my love."

I caressed her body, following a path of water, traveling to her feet. With all of the rain showerheads across the ceiling, it was like we were in an enclosed rainforest. We were surrounded by water. I reached to turn off one head, closest to the wall, just before I lay her down on the marble floor. I grabbed a pillow from the sitting area, and placed it under her head. I planted kisses all over her wet body. She arched her back and I put my arms under her, as she opened her legs. Her moisture mixed with shower water, as my tongue tasted her dainties. She moaned and swelled with pleasure. My mind cleared and made room to be consumed by my wife's eroticism. She ran her fingers through my hair and gently held my head in place.

"Right there, Morris." She whispered. "Yes, lover, that's it." Her hips had a mind of their own, as she sought her pleasure.

I could hear my cell phone ringing, in the bedroom, but I ignored it, sensing her heightened arousal. She would come soon, and I never interrupt. I focused on my wife and I was rewarded with a deep moan, during her orgasm. It was strong, and left her trembling. I entered her, just as she began to catch her breath.

Once we had our fill, I stood, helping her to her feet. I reached for a sponge to wash her aroused body. She shuddered, as I paid special attention to her breasts and buttocks. She reciprocated and we stepped out of the shower, and wrapped ourselves in heated towels.

I reached for her favorite lotion, applying it to her body. "I love the afterglow of our lovemaking, on your skin."

"You handle me, so well." She purred.

"I am glad to hear that, my love."

The phone rang, again.

"It must be important, at this hour."

"It certainly better be." I said, as I reached for the phone.

SARAH YOUNG

I missed my husband's affection. I did not know if this is better than my parent's relationship. Kenneth was brooding and darker every day. He was not abusive to me. He was, simply, leaving me to myself. He locked himself away for hours on end. And when he was not in his office, he was out. When he returned, he looked like he had been in a brawl. He came home with blood splatters on his clothes and sweat pouring from his brow. He resembled a man tormented by evil spirits, paranoid and violent. I did not try to imagine things he was doing, while away. I breathed a sigh of relief, when he showered and went to his study to sit and stare. At least, he was not coming to our bed with anger corralled in his soul.

I could hear him pacing the floor, through the night, as if he was always restless. He had been having effusive episodes since Jacqueline left home to marry Morris, but they were becoming more frequent since her death and funeral. He would disappear for hours, but I thought it was for prayer and meditation. He was edgy about black people who decided to attend church and subsequent haranguing from his fellows in the pastorate. He was under pressure.

I did my best to soothe him, during some darker moments, but he didn't accept my comfort. He was inconsolable. I was afraid he would turn his grief to rage and attack me, as my father often did to my mother. When he rejected attempts, I hurried out of the room to safety of bedroom, locking the door. I tried to pray for him and our family. I did not know what to say to God allowing tragedy to befall us. Where had divine protection been when that animal brutalized Jacqueline? Kenneth preached of our power over the races, yet the Wells family was alive and our daughter is dead.

I had to keep this lack of desire to pray to myself. No one would understand how I got here. My husband is pastor of a fairly large church. We are upstanding citizens, respected by many. What would they think, knowing Kenneth's soul was dark as a sin, deserving hell's punishment? How judgmental would the ladies, of my circle, be if they found out I didn't have faith to pray for my husband, or family?

I got up from the chair and approached the window, as I heard the front door close. I saw Kenneth head to his car. I gasped. I could swear I saw a skulking apparition close to him, pushing him with talon-like claws. I closed my eyes and opened them, quickly. He was already in the car, but the apparition sat low on the hood, billowing wispy clouds, holding on to the sides.

"Dear God!" I covered my mouth in shock. "What is happening to my husband?"

PRESTON LAMBERT

I sent Morris a lot of information, and words God gave me to share. I did not want him to get bored learning about the Lord and what He desired for his life. I sensed a spiritual war, in the atmosphere.

I remembered my grandmother, Mother Salester, talking about spiritual warfare taking place in the heavenlies. *We do not wrestle with flesh and blood, but against principalities and powers of air.* I could not discern if the attack was directed toward my family or that of Morris, but I would get on my post and pray, in the Spirit. I decided it best if Damaris and I took up this charge. We were able to dismantle the enemy's plans, on several occasions.

We would use scriptures to pray against things from pasts and that of our family and friends. I remembered Corinthians 5:17, *"Anyone who belongs to Christ is a new person. The past is forgotten, and everything is new."* When Christ died, He took pasts of all to the grave. We would meditate on the idea, let it roll around in our spirits. We took into account all that was happening. We contemplated God's goodness, which is almost too wonderful to comprehend its depth, length and height.

In my letter to Morris, I encouraged him to think about Colossians 3:3:

"For you died, and your life is now hidden with Christ in God. Many of us walk around begrudging our pasts. We hold on to things we have done, not forgiving ourselves. We are bitter toward those who have hurt us, and bitter about the pain we endured. We think our lives were unlike someone else's and no one can understand. Anyone who belongs to Christ is a new person. The past is forgotten, and everything is new."

I wrote Morris that everyone wants a second opportunity. Some long to start over. I assured him Christ gave him that chance; he should take Him up on that part of deliverance.

"We should always remember what Christ did. We should not just think about Him saving us from hell. He saved us from our pasts and everything that is associated with it. We will benefit most if we just let it go. He took it to the cross. By His stripes,

we are healed. In His body, He took our pain and wrong deeds. Whom the Son sets free, is free indeed. Our past has no hold on us, unless we pick it up and carry it. It doesn't benefit us to hold our pasts against us, or that of others against them. If we put off that 'old man', then we gain more by accepting His sacrifice for our lives."

I, also, included an article my pastor wrote for a notable Christian magazine, entitled, *YOU ARE ON HIS MIND.* Pastor began with Jeremiah 29:11. *"For I know the plans I have for you, declares the LORD, plans to prosper you and not to harm you, plans to give you hope and a future."* I believe there are some of us, within the Body of Christ, who have a hard time with this. We quote it. We get warm feelings when we hear it. However, how many of us take comfort in it, when we are in the throes of fiery trials and circumstances? How many of us take comfort in it, when our pasts have been difficult to bear? How many of us set it to our souls to keep bitterness from creeping into our lives?"

I included a prayer from Damaris. She wanted to let Morris know she is on his side and loves the person he is becoming. She was captivated by his thirst for things of God and wanted him to be encouraged.

Father, You have sovereign rule of heaven and earth. We are Your sheep. You called and chose us to walk in freedom wrought by Your blood. The sacrifice You made allows us to come, boldly, to Your throne of grace. We walk in Your mercy, daily. We are infused by love You share, as You have purposed for us to share of Your goodness. For that, we are thankful. You want to be known, by us; we are fully known, and You hid Yourself in secret of our search. You said knock and the door would open. You said, seek and we will find. You said, draw near to You and You will draw near to us.

Lord, let our heart's cry to know You. Help us be genuine and less vocal in vacant promises. You are not concerned in our sacrifices, time we take to pray, or read or give. You are interested in condition of our heart and how we choose to turn it over to You. A broken and contrite heart, You will never turn away.

We are not worthy, so You filled us with Yourself and called us holy, because You are holy. We can love You, because You have loved us and are a perfect example. You loved us enough to give, so we give ourselves to You. We cry out of our spirits, ABBA! And expect You to wrap us, in the safety of Your arms. We will bless Your name and magnify You above everything, else. We will not focus on what You have not called us to focus. We will find the lovely, pure and praiseworthy thing, in our lives, and think on those things. We will cast down, every vain imagination trying to exalt itself against knowledge of You, and in turn, we look to You to give us clean hands, words and thoughts.

Lord, I come to You, today, on behalf of Your child. Father, You are concerned and intricately at work on behalf of my brother. You dispatched angels to succor him, on the path You chose. He belongs to You; he is Your son, beloved, and apple of Your eye. You love him, and Your plan for his life is to prosper him. Help him to govern his affairs in a manner pleasing to You.

You are the Balm in Gilead, easing and removing pain upon his spirit. Teach him Your ways, speak to his heart, and give him spiritual peace that surpasses thought. Give him dreams and visions. Send him encouraging words, whenever he feels like he isn't making strides to move closer to You. Bolster his confidence, whenever he has to stand for hard right against easy wrong. Give him the strength to conquer habits that hinder the next move You have planned. Give him many reasons to smile, as You hold his hand through this journey.

Lord, love him, as he reads this prayer. I bless You for his life, health and strength. You are worthy of praise, glory and honor, yet if we had a million tongues, we would never do You justice.

Thank You for inclining Your ear to hear voice of our supplications and preparing a way to give us desires of our heart. You are awesome! I pray this and believe it to be done, according to the power you have given to me by the name of your Son, Jesus; it is so! AMEN!!!

MORRIS WELLS, SR.

He must pay. My ire was kindled since the call, the other night. I held an emergency meeting with Keyvaughn and business associates to discuss options. On the one hand, there was good news; on the other, an enemy needed to be addressed. We decided to let natural progression take course. We would present evidence to authorities and let chips fall.

Patricia filled with venom as I told her the news. Anger quickly replaced a lovemaking afterglow. Patricia wanted swift vengeance and retribution for the ones who brought such sadness to our family. I quieted her with kisses and assurances that fast justice would be served.

Keyvaughn had to employ control when he heard the news. He fought against regret for not taking matters into his own hands sooner. I reminded him that had he done what he desired, we would not be able to do anything about our situation. We would have been in stalemate that did not benefit us. With matters as they were, we would get what we want. Revenge is best served cold. He will not know what is coming.

"With all the players dealt with, this could have been difficult to prove." I said.

"They had to be taken care of for betrayal and lack of follow-through. If not, things could have become critical."

"I am not regretting our move, son. I am just grateful it did not prevent us from seeking truth."

We gave details to newly hired lawyers and awaited the next move. I am not a patient man when it comes to my family. The new attorneys had to learn our dynamic and how to maneuver within those confines. We demanded a hundred percent success.

The phone rang and I walked across the room to retrieve it. I listened, intently, and scribbled down a few notes to pass on to Keyvaughn. I smiled once the conversation was over. We would have what we wanted, in a matter of days.

The proverbial ball was rolling.

KENNETH YOUNG

My mind was more distressed as months passed. I was withdrawn from church duty, and as a husband and father. I was sure it had to do with contact with the blacks. I felt like a werewolf, in those horror films, I wanted to rip and tear flesh off of those barbarians. I tried to pick up the bible. I needed to clear my head, yet I was more confused and troubled. I placed the book on the shelf and clicked on the television.

I saw a breaking news story, so I turned up the volume. I saw reporters and police officers in front of the jail in our area. I saw the new district attorney, mayor and a gaggle of lawyers. There was a makeshift podium. A press conference took place.

"What an interesting turn of events." One reporter said.

"Morris Wells, Jr. is being released from Norfolk jail after shocking evidence points to a trail of blackmail and false dealings. It was brought to the district attorney's office several office members falsified conviction. A Supreme Court judge overturned ruling in Morris Wells' case, as new proof

implicates another person in the murder of Jacqueline Wells, the defendant's wife. We are not at liberty to divulge the name of the new suspect, as the party has not been taken into custody." The leader spoke.

I was raging. I could barely breathe, as its choking presence rose. I slammed my fist on my desk, with such ferocity that items toppled over, some broke into pieces. I looked at the shards from my fallen lamp scattered on the floor, and felt my psyche follow suit. I was deranged in my wrath. I couldn't hear words, from the television. All I could see was the Wells family smiling and welcoming their loved one back into the fold. My Jacqueline is dead because of them. Those niggers must pay for causing my daughter's demise. I opened my desk drawer and pulled out a revolver that I purchased a few weeks ago. I placed it in my briefcase and then headed to my office door. Something caught my eye, outside of my window.

It was the police.

SARAH YOUNG

There was an incessant banging on the door. I hurried from the kitchen to see who could have been causing such a raucous. I did not want the noise to disturb Kenneth. I heard what sounded like his fist hitting his desk, breaking glass, and then silence. As I neared the door, I realized there were police cruisers in our driveway and officers at the door. What happened now? Fear crept in, causing my hairs to stand on end. I couldn't move. I was frozen.

I expected Kenneth to storm out of the office and ask me what was going on down here and why was I taking so long to answer the door. There was nothing, just banging. After a few more thuds, there was a loud crash. Wood splinters filled the air and officers rushed in. I heard them talking, but I could not comprehend what was being said.

"Ma'am, we're looking for Kenneth Young. Can you tell me where he is?" One officer spoke to me. "Ma'am, can you hear me?"

I felt someone shaking me, attempting to rouse me from stupor. Yet, all I could do was stare, blankly, as they searched all of the rooms on the bottom floor.

"We have a warrant for the arrest of Mr. Kenneth Young for murder of Jacqueline Wells." An officer screamed my direction.

Several officers ran up the stairs, when I heard a loud popping sound.

"Shots have been fired from one of the rooms up here." A tall officer yelled.

I turned to look up, still not fully cognizant of the situation. I saw them push their way into Kenneth's office.

"A man shot himself in the head, Captain. He appears to be dead."

Everything went black.

EPILOGUE

Mother Salester's death hit Preston and his family like a ton of bricks. They were still recovering from their patriarch, Joseph Lambert death, and now they faced more shocking loss. Kathleen, Preston's mother, took it hardest. Her relationship with her mother-in-law was incredible. They were like mother and daughter. After death of her son, Mother Salester remained in close contact with her and even moved in with her when she had a difficult moment.

Preston's siblings, Aaron and Anise, were silent, which was unlike the twins. Both of them were outgoing and outspoken. Tamu, Aaron's longtime girlfriend, stuck close to him. The same went for Anise's husband, Desmond. He took his station by his wife's side. He took care of their two-year old, David, while she came to terms with the senseless act of violence.

Mother Salester was with a church group, The Silver Years, on an evangelism outing in an affluent area. No one expected such opposition and certainly not to the point of murdering an elderly woman, offering the love of Christ. The murder occurred in daylight, the murderer had no regret as he resolutely dumped her body on a sidewalk.

Damaris was praying, desperately, for her husband. The Lamberts were closer than any family she knew and she felt blessed to be a part of the family. Mother Salester was Preston's heart. They shared so many things. She gave him the nod of approval when approached about their relationship.

"I know God shared something with you. Do not doubt it and do not be afraid. You are ready, son. He gave you everything you need to be a success and blessing. I pray God sees fit to allow me to live long enough to share in the good thing He has prepared for you." Mother Salester shed joyful tears, as she reached her arms out to her eldest grandson, that day.

Damaris was grateful for the impact, which Mother Salester had on Preston that day, as it gave him the courage to believe what he had been hearing God say about their relationship. She loved her husband with a deep and abiding affection. He was a good man and she was concerned with how this would to affect him. There were moments where Preston went inward. She trusted God would safeguard her husband's spirit, but it was hard to see him so sad.

As the family sat with friends, everyone watched the news as the murderer was escorted into the police station.

"Keyvaughn Wells turned himself in to the authorities earlier today. His lawyer staved off reporters and passersby."

Preston leaned forward, as a close-up of the accused appeared on screen. His brow furrowed and his jaw clenched.

"He looks oddly familiar." He whispered.

Micah, Preston's long time friend, leaned in as well. "I can see what you're saying."

"Do you, two, know this man?" Kathleen asked, incredulously.

"I don't recall meeting him, but I might know someone who resembles him."

"He looks a lot like Morris, Preston." Micah replied, after a moment.

"Morris Wells...the fellow God led you to in the prison ministry?" Damaris asked.

Preston sat still, for a long moment. "Yes, the young man that I had the honor of leading to Christ."

The reporter was speaking, so they turned up the volume. "Mr. Wells is a successful engineer and comes from a well respected family of professionals. Most noteworthy of them is Morris Wells, wrongly accused of murdering his wife, Jacqueline Wells."

News of the connection silenced the room.